JUST PLAIN FOLKS

JUST PLAIN FOLKS

Original Tales
of Living, Loving, Longing, and Learning,
As Told by a Perfectly Ordinary,
Quite Commonly Sensible,
and Absolutely Awe-Inspiring
Colored Woman

LORRAINE JOHNSON-COLEMAN

LITTLE, BROWN AND COMPANY

Boston New York Toronto London

A different version of this book was published in hardcover
by Summerhouse Press, 1997
First edition, revised

ISBN 0-316-46084-2

Library of Congress Catalog Card Number 98-66934

10   9   8   7   6   5   4   3   2   1

MV-NY

Published simultaneously in Canada by Little, Brown & Company
(Canada) Limited

Printed in the United States of America

This book is dedicated to my husband,
Lance Coleman,
and my four small children,
Larissa, Lauren, Lance, Jr., and Latrice,
whom I love with all my heart.

LISTEN MY CHILE

I know you think you been raised 'cause you grown now
but a mama always got to wonder
what else can I say to my child who is black?
I know what you're thinking
She's been talkin' my whole life,
it's time to let well enough alone, to trust me, to let me be,
but you know your mama, and I couldn't rest,
not even with the Lord hisself,
if I thought I left my task unfinished or even one word unsaid.
Did I tell you that no matter how tough the task,
how high the steps, or how hard the journey,
it's OK to get weary? — but you ain't walkin' this walk alone.
You always got my footprints to guide you
'cause I been down this road before.
Now I know your feet ain't mine
and we can't step into the same shoes
and I know too you gonna find your own way —
all I'm saying is that you ain't by yourself.

Have I told you I'm sorry
'cause I wasn't always the one who lifted you when you fell,
healed you when you ached, or helped you when you hurt?
But sometimes making that way out of no way just took all I had.
Every once in a while I had to leave the mothering
to God's own guardian angels — them other mamas,
the aunties, the sisters, the grannies and the nannies —
but you know you was loved
and chile, I'll always be your mama.
Chile, I been granny to yours,
Mama to mine,
Mother to the motherless,
and missus to my man,
but I never stopped being my own woman.
I got feet that been trampled, and blisters on my blisters,
but I can still kick up the dust, walk a mean high-heel strut,
and cross my legs with the uppitiest of women on a
first Sunday morn.
Chile, no matter how tough things get —
and they gonna get mighty tough —
You got to keep going. You ain't gonna make it
stopping short or standing still.
Sometimes being a woman is so tough,
you gonna feel like you trying to dance on quicksand
or catch up to the moon
but trouble's always coming, and you can't stop it
no more than you can hold back the tears
or sweep up the ocean with a raggedy old broom.
But you gonna make it, the Father above told me it would be true.
'Sides, I wouldn't be looking for nothing less
'Cause I'm expecting at least that much out of you.

— Mama

Contents

Introduction   xi
Kinfolks

Journeys Home   3

Call Me by My Name   13

Sorrow's Kitchen   24

The Freedom Garden   33

Homefolks

One of the Homegrown Angels   47

Gettin' Ready   58

Three Sixes   73

Every Other Tuesday Off   79

Women and Men Folks

Hitched   91

Sophie with the Gold Tooth   98

Miz Lullabel, the Devil, and the Sunday Hat   109

Lost Love, Last Love   118

The Bluesman   125

One Uppity Blues Woman   130

Contents

Young Folks

The Colored Water Fountain   139

Nobody's Chile   144

Hush-a-Bye   147

Little Boy Blue   153

Little Cinder Lea   156

Willy Did It   164

White Folks

White Folks   181

Hagar's Children   186

Sara's Precious Babies   192

And the People of a Town Go Round and Round   199

Church Folks

Sister Mabel   213

Brother Jake   219

Mister Jim   224

The Reverend   228

A Final Say   235

Acknowledgments   241

Introduction

I think that I must have gone through my midlife crisis very early in life. I was only thirty at the time. It's the only explanation that I can come up with for wanting to turn my comfortable middle-class existence upside down. I started looking at the things that had been a part of my thinking for years, and suddenly they weren't making sense. I'd always appreciated my African American ethnicity — that was never an issue. It was just that suddenly my understanding of this thing called heritage wasn't adding up to what it was supposed to, and I couldn't understand why. I'd read the appropriate books, studied the available literature. I knew all the significant dates and places that any aware and progressive-thinking African American was supposed to know. I took the right history courses in college and even managed to memorize the "I Have a Dream" speech. I went to all the black history programs I could, but I watched with growing annoyance as we talked about those same twelve or so black folks who supposedly made up *all* of our history.

To the outside world, it appeared as if I were progressing along a preordained path, and it would be only a matter of time before I was a contributing member of some prestigious African American civil-rights or social organization. That was the plan, but the path took an unexpected turn.

Because my roots are Southern, I had a particular interest in the heritage that comes from that part of the country. Despite what I was being taught, Southern history for African Americans had to consist of more than the brutality of slavery and the struggle for civil rights. There had to be more folks and diverse events in there somewhere — more interesting communities, more stories, celebrations, and triumphs in the middle of the historical struggle that I'd studied.

There was a reason that at the most upscale African American events, collard greens were usually served. And I can well remember that in the midst of some of the most educated and formal presentations, there was usually a lapse, be it momentarily, into a li'l homegrown wisdom like "tell the truth and shame the Devil." There appeared to be a great deal more to this heritage talk than anyone was saying, and I was determined to find out what it was. Zora Neal Hurston and her work provided the first glimmers of evidence. I figured there should be someone new to pick up her torch and run with it, so I made that my mission.

The journey into this understanding began five years ago, and it hasn't been an easy trip. It has taken me to some places I had never before imagined, and to some places

I've always known. It allowed me to meet some people I could never completely describe, but could never forget, either. It required that I stop *playing* a proud African American and really *become* one, as I came to realize that three hundred years of black history rested squarely on my shoulders. And that means history as it relates to our experiences in *this* country and understanding how these are indeed linked back to the motherland. So I have come to appreciate that worn headrag and what it has meant for us as a people as much as I celebrate that kinte cloth and its ever-growing significance in our communities.

I really did think I had made it, or at least was on my way, when I became a happily married, successful, and somewhat well-educated woman. I didn't realize that making it was still a long way away. I would still need to touch the hearts and souls of some black women from the past and then try to understand what *they* understood in order to be any kind of decent woman today. It really wasn't enough to be an African American woman — I would also have to be comfortable with being a perfectly ordinary, quite commonly sensible, and absolutely awe-inspiring colored woman before I could possibly come close to succeeding the way my grandmamas had done. I would need their truths, their honesty, and the kind of faith that can come only from another time.

At last, I found the kind of wisdom I'd been searching for in Farmville, North Carolina, the ancestral home of my kinfolks — amid the cottonfields, tobacco barns, and dilapidated shacks. It started there, but I quickly began branching out. I went to other rural places and talked to even more folks, and I graciously accepted all that they were willing to give, and they gave me so much. They let me in, allowed me to borrow their kin, lifted me so I could peek over their shoulders, inspired me to listen to their stories, and looked the other way as I stole some of their secrets. By the time my research was done, I had more good stuff than I could ever share word-for-word, so I took it all in, added a lot of imagination, and then expressed it as best I could in my very own way. These stories are the result of that effort.

It would be rude and irresponsible to take folks' valuables and then just leave them vulnerable to harm or danger. It's the same with these tales of living, loving, and learning. I have told the story, yes, in a way that I am quite proud of, but I am also smart enough to realize that that is not nearly enough. There is still the possibility of misinterpretation despite the best of intentions on both our parts, and I didn't want that to happen. So, after each story or section, I have added a short essay that allows these stories to be placed within a proper cultural perspective.

I have surely been blessed, I know that. But blessings are no good to anyone unless you pass them on. I've had the good fortune of being taken through the back door of the most personal of places by some really good folks. These are diverse experiences here, and I don't want you to miss a single one. Some of these stories make you feel "oh so good," and others, well, they force you to swallow down some sorrow or hold back some rage. But then again, isn't experiencing all of those kinds of feelings what living is all about?

Kinfolks

Journeys Home

It was trying miserably to be inconspicuous, failing in its attempts to be subtle with its demands and softspoken with its commands. The beautiful beige envelope had been tossed casually on the kitchen table with the rest of the day's mail, but even in the midst of the many, it was arrogant in its presence, insisting that I devote my full and immediate attention to it. I moved the other letters aside and slowly picked it up. It was that time of year again, and I knew it even before my eyes could fully focus on the elegant raised lettering. Mama at her best, I thought, as I slowly opened the invitation — calligraphy, vellum paper, and even a tissue liner. A little much given the nature of the occasion, but no one ever could tell Mama a thing.

The invitation was clean, crisp, and straight to the point — clear evidence of Mama's no-nonsense style. All this show and no little extras — not even a short Bible verse or a thought-provoking lead-in. Not one to waste energy on the nonessential, Mama believed that if you had something to say, you just took careful aim, spat it out, and let it land where it may.

> *The Burney-Green Family*
> *cordially invite you to their annual*
> *Family Reunion*
> *at the homestead.*

No address was given, not that one was really necessary. We all knew the place. No need to read any further. I knew the date, and I was sure of the time. Some things are about as regular, inevitable, and bittersweet as the ending of summer's long, lazy days — like a good daughter's obligations; like a family reunion.

I wondered if, since I am a member of the Burney-Green family, technically this meant I had sent an invitation to myself. Lord, who was I kidding? This was none of my doing. These were clearly the markings of a queen mother, and there was nothing cordial about it. Although not actually printed on those breathtaking sheets, the message was quite clear, the summons quite specific, and the tone really quite firm: Be there!

Farmville, North Carolina, is down east near Goldsboro, round 'bout Greenville, and a holler from Snowhill. Like the folks who live there, it lays kinship claim to just about anything near it. There was a sprinkling of newly constructed homes among the now deteriorating wooden ones. On this visit I noticed they had added one extra stoplight downtown, and some of the stores had been given a facelift. At one time there had even been talk of adding a strip mall and a new hotel right on the outskirts of town, but so far nothing concrete had materialized. Other than these few "progressive" changes, Farmville looked just like it had the year before. That was fine with me, though. It was comforting to know that Farmville was there when I needed it, and right where I'd left it, despite the fact that I had moved miles beyond it.

Farmville welcomed me in its usual August way, a greeting with sunshine so bright, a heat so hugging, and humidity so mugging it could set your carefully curled head all the way back to its natural kinky nap. The tar-licked roads seem to stretch on endlessly, like the lazy summer afternoon. The old folks were sitting on the front porch, waving me on with one hand and swatting flies with the other. The overgrown gardens that used to provide pickings for a full year now just rambled aimlessly until they met up with a mile-high cornfield. Even the pungent smell of tobacco seemed as strong and familiar as a musty old friend. There were no street signs way out in the country — just follow the shallow ditch 'cross the railroad track, pass on by the Williamses' old drinking well, go beyond H. B. Suggs Training School, turn right at the Holiness Church, and proceed a quarter mile straight ahead to the homestead.

It was only eight o'clock Saturday morning. Most of the family wouldn't be arriving until much later in the afternoon, in time for the fish fry. Only the planning-committee members were required to be here this early. This was the first year that a "young'un" (young at age thirty?) was allowed to serve among the illustrious group, and fortunate or not, I was the chosen. No one was here yet. That was good. It was a definite point in my favor that

5

I took my duties so seriously that I was the first to arrive. I wondered if Aunt Maribelle would acknowledge the fact and give me my due.

The entourage began arriving at nine o'clock. I had been sitting in my car, trying desperately to sleep but mostly engaged in active combat with the relentless Carolina mosquitoes and gnats, which could flesh out fresh meat and swarm with a vengeance. It was a losing battle. I was just about to call it quits and leave when I spotted Uncle Alvesta's pickup pulling in next to my car. As usual, he slammed the door to announce his arrival, stumbled, and then kicked the dirt as if it had somehow offended him. At fifty-five, he was of average height, somewhat pudgy, very thick around the middle, with a pleasant enough face and a grin that reeked of so much mischief you always wondered what he had just been up to. He had more money than God, but he was a simple man. He always wore black hard-toed shoes, dark-blue work pants, and a short-sleeved cotton shirt. His missions in life were to make even more money, to be the best electrician in Washington, D.C., and to cook the family-reunion pig.

"Hey, cotton picker," he said with a smirk, kicking dirt on my brand-new sneakers and arrogantly waiting for me to rise to the bait. I have never picked cotton, I shouted at him silently. He's my mother's brother, I reminded myself as I shuffled my feet to knock off the excess dirt.

"Hey, Uncle, where's the rest of the family?" I even forced a smile that was probably a bit too wide. I figured out for myself that my cousins probably didn't want to hear his mouth for six straight hours. One thing for sure: my cousins had plenty of sense.

"They'll be here later, in time for the fish fry. Hey, what's up? Ain't nobody here yet?" (What was I, chopped liver?)

"Apparently not. Oh, spoke too soon. Here comes Aunt Maribelle."

Aunt Maribelle must have scooted out of the car in some kind of hurry because she was already halfway 'cross the yard, and Uncle Milton was still trying to open his door. Not easy moving that fast when you're carrying a ten-gallon pot of, my guess, collard greens. Why we couldn't make Aunt Maribelle understand that it wasn't necessary to cook greens in New York and drag 'em halfway 'cross the country was beyond me. She had probably convinced herself that if she didn't bring them with her, one of us "young'uns," in a fit of madness, would probably run down the road to one of the local black caterers who made greens just as good as Aunt Maribelle's and sold 'em so cheap it would save a lot of trouble. The idea had merit, but not to Aunt Maribelle. Her greens, and her greens alone, would be served at the family reunion, and that, as they say, was that.

At sixty-four, Aunt Maribelle was short and stout, with a youthful face that had cheekbones so high and so wide there was no room for wrinkles. She had a beautiful head of thick, healthy hair, and when she was so inclined, she could do wonders with a jar of grease, a hot comb, and a lot of too-tight curls, strategically placed all over her head in untouchable, neat, even rows. Unfortunately, she rarely had the inclination. Instead, she usually wore a wig that looked like she had thrown it up in the air, closed her eyes, and waited for it to land any which way it wanted to on the top of her head. Today she must have dressed in the dark. She was wearing one of those "work dresses" — the hem was torn, and the dress hung raggedly around her legs. She hadn't bothered to put on stockings, but instead wore knee-highs. I knew this because they didn't quite make it to her knees, but clung midcalf in fierce desperation. She was a very sweet person most of the time, and the rest — oh well, you can't pick your relatives.

"Hey, Alvesta," Aunt Maribelle cried out, "Garland called and said he's going to be tied up all day, so I guess you and I got to get this thing together. We better get started 'cause we've got a lot to do." She turned to me at last.

"Good morning, Daughter." Since she only had one son, she called all sixteen of her nieces "Daughter." It was meant to be a term of endearment, but it could also sound like a reprimand. Today it came across as an afterthought.

She shoved the big pot of greens into my hands and gave me the unspoken directions to put it into the "frizerator." I was starting to figure that this young'un's responsibilities for the day were to do as told, ask very few questions, and do very little planning. This was going to be a long weekend.

I looked around the kitchen after I put the pot away. The black iron stove had been there at least fifty years. The floor was warped, and the linoleum had started to venture in its own direction and curl inward. It might have been yellow once, but over time, countless footsteps had worn it almost black. There were islands of bright spots that still lingered, remnants of beauty refusing to be forgotten. The entire house was not supposed to have made it. It had been built by folks who didn't know where their next dollar was coming from. It hadn't been designed for a family of twelve, either, but it held them, all very near and very, very dear. Despite the hardship of being a "colored folks' dwelling" in a town determined to make it prove its worthiness and fortitude day after day, it had performed its duties honorably.

There was no shame here, I thought as I surveyed the humble surroundings. Sharecroppers had dragged bone-weary bodies through these narrow doors, and the house had been here for them, arms open wide and a pillar of strength to lean on. Everybody always had a warm bed in which to rest a bit, and, thank you Lord, even with a shelf full of nothing, no one ever went hungry. These very windowsills had once held mason jars full of nickels that had, amazingly, put four Burneys through college. No, there was no shame here. Not even in the midst of the decay, the piecemeal patchwork, and the much-needed mendings. Some would say it was past its prime, but I realized it was a testament that transcended time. No, there was no shame here.

It was becoming clear to me. This was what it was all about — black history in the making. Not just the often-repeated facts, but the genuinely heartfelt feelings. I was a little ashamed of myself. I had planned to use my "influence" on the planning committee to suggest that we move the family reunion next year to a community center near Greenville with a caterer and a live band. It was just so difficult coming back year after year now that Aunt Bessida was no longer here and neither was Grandpa. It was hard to look at the old oak tree out back and not remember that it was where he sat every day for forty years — that tree that he told all of his dreams to, amid the shadows where he buried all of his troubles.

Now I'd changed my mind about suggesting we move the reunion. I guess no matter how hard you try or how far you run, you really can't leave your loved ones behind. Not even in Greenville, in a community center.

My thoughts were interrupted by Uncle Alvesta, who threw at least one hundred pounds of fish in the sink right in front of me. I jumped back so I wouldn't be drenched in the process.

"Uncle Alvesta, what are you doing?"

"This is the fish for the fish fry."

"Well, couldn't you have had them cleaned at the docks? They do that, you know, for just a couple of pennies a fish. Who's supposed to clean all these fish?" I didn't realize it, but I must have been screaming, because Aunt Maribelle came running in so fast you would have thought I'd announced that the house was on fire.

"Daughter, we always clean the fish ourselves, that way we know they're clean." She wiped her hands on a rag she had tied around her waist. (I always give her an apron every year for Christmas. I wonder what she does with them.) "Here, let me show you." Her impatience was showing. "You clean 'em underwater. Slice the head off, slit it down the middle, clear out all the guts, and scale it. It won't take us more than a couple of hours. Really, Daughter!" There it was, that "Daughter" that sounded like a cuss word.

Someone once said, "The family is one of nature's masterpieces," but I wondered, as I rolled up my shirtsleeves and grabbed one particularly large, very slimy fish, if whoever it was had an Aunt Maribelle or an Uncle Alvesta.

AFTERTHOUGHTS

I was fortunate recently to have the opportunity to work with a science museum on the creation of an exhibition of African American inventiveness. As I toured the final showcasing, I couldn't help but feel an incredible sense of pride in the men and women whose work was on display. This was true genius! We were aware, of course, that we had but touched the surface of the vast arena called "inventiveness," but let's face it, we had limited space. Then, I didn't realize how much of the story there was left to tell, but now I know that inventiveness goes way beyond the *Webster's Dictionary* definition of "originating a product out of individual ingenuity." I strongly feel that inventiveness can also include the resourcefulness of a people. I think it's that very resourcefulness, the ability to make do and get it done, that we celebrate at each and every family reunion.

My granddaddy would surely smile if he knew that the modest little wooden house that we all called the "homeplace" is now known in academic circles as an example of vernacular architecture. A vernacular structure is not built from detailed blueprints or by formally trained hands, but rather created from the blood, sweat, and tears of simple folks who use only hand-me-down knowledge about how best to keep the wind and rain off your back.

How I love that humble dwelling place, that simple little shack where Granddaddy lived. With its cozy familiarity, its worn interiors, and its sharecroppers past, it seems to me to be the grandest of places. It was filled with the enormity of ordinary folks and their never-ending dreams. No matter how fine our homes were in the North, they took a backseat to that place in Carolina that connected us to something larger and more significant than ourselves. I know how lucky I am. It seems like some folks have to search the world over to find themselves, but I have never been lost. I simply have to keep my eye on a little white house in the heart of Farmville, North Carolina.

Call Me by My Name

"Lorraine Harriet." I said the name with all the authority I could muster, speaking directly to my reflection in the bedroom mirror. Still wasn't right.

"Lorraine Harriet." I said it this time in a sexy whisper like the perfume models I'd seen on television. Nope, still wasn't right; sexy just didn't go with the thirteen-year-old face looking back at me.

"Lorraine Harriet." I pronounced it with my best Southern drawl, dragging each syllable on round the room and back again. Even worse; the name just didn't fit, hanging loosely around me like one of my cousins' baggy hand-me-down outfits hanging in the hall closet. The Lorraine wasn't too bad; not so common that you ran into yourself coming and going, and different enough that it had a touch of class. It was the Harriet. Who in the world would put Harriet next to Lorraine? "Your mother," the mirror answered back.

My mother had probably still been groggy when the nurse came around and asked her what she wanted on the

13

birth certificate. After all, she had just had twins and must not have been too with it at the time. What other explanation could there be for such poor judgment? Surely she hadn't been thinking of the future, the day a thirteen-year-old girl would have to pick this name up and try carrying it around. When you're little, it doesn't matter, but when you're thirteen, that's another story. Thirteen-year-olds have enough problems without trying to squeeze into a name that just doesn't fit.

Loretta Doris, my twin sister, was standing by the bed, putting the last few items in the suitcase. This was the first year we had been allowed to shop for and pack our own clothes for the family reunion. Loretta had decided to do the packing for both of us to be sure we would be ready on time. I wondered if Loretta gave any thought to the fit of her name? Nah! Loretta wasn't one to give second thoughts to things that already were. She slammed the suitcase closed with smug satisfaction.

"Lorraine Harriet." I sang it this time like a lyrical Sunday hymn. Nope, even Jesus and the Holy Spirit couldn't help this name. If my sister was wondering why I was walking around saying my name like a broken record, she didn't say anything — just walked out of the room to gather together the toiletries.

Once I'd asked my mother why she had chosen these names for us.

"Loretta and Lorraine seemed like cute twin names," she said.

"But why the Harriet and Doris? That's where you went wrong."

"I named you after my mother, Harriet, who died on

Christmas Day when I was only sixteen years old," she said. "And of course, Loretta is named after me." I felt a little better after the explanation, but I still couldn't help wondering if the after-birth grogginess might not have had something to do with it.

We left New York later that evening and traveled all night, finally arriving in Farmville just before breakfast. Bone-tired and dead on our feet, we wanted nothing more than a soft, warm bed and a few hours' sleep. Aunt Maribelle, Aunt Bessida, and Uncle Garland were seated at the table having a Saturday breakfast Farmville style: fish and grits. The fish were fried golden brown and smelled delicious. The grits had been sprinkled with cheese, and there was a big plate of cornbread in the center of the table. Maybe I wasn't so sleepy after all — a quick shower and a change of clothes woke me up enough to face the family.

Aunt Bessida Lee. There were lots of Lees 'round Farmville. It was one of those names that popped up a lot — like Mae. I guess when you're busy having twelve and fifteen children, there isn't time to be creative. Just find a good solid name and tag along a Lee or a Mae and be done with it. Easy.

Now Aunt Maribelle, that one was a little off the beaten path, and Garland was one for the books. It sounded like a fantasy forest or a state park. Grandma must have really been out of it when she came up with that one.

Aunt Bessida's two sons, Will Alvesta and George William, came into the kitchen just as I was reaching for a plate. Better hurry, I thought, or the two of them will polish off the whole stack of fried fish. Those boys could really eat. Will Alvesta had been named Will for his father and

15

Alvesta for my uncle Alvesta. That fit 'cause he had the same sneaky grin as Uncle Alvesta. Now, George William was named after my grandpa George. That worked, too, 'cause he was quiet and thoughtful like Grandpa. As for the William, I wasn't sure.

Now, in the South there are a lot of women named Sis and, oh yeah, a lot named Baby — lots and lots of them. Nicknames are so common here that they don't even have to make any sense. Once I met this little boy out in Grandpa's yard when I was about six. He looked like he had good possibilities for a playmate, so I hurried to catch up to him before he crossed over to his yard. He was holding a little boy by the hand who looked to be about three years old.

"What's your name?" I screamed to stop him in his tracks. "Mine's Lorraine!"

"Name's Noah Junior, but everybody calls me Jimmy."

"If your name is Noah, why do they call you Jimmy?"

"Just do."

"What's his name?" I asked, pointing to the chubby three-year-old, who was staring at me like I had something stuck in my teeth.

"He ain't got a name. We just call him B.B."

"B.B.?"

"Yeah. Baby Boy."

"Baby Boy! You mean he don't have a real name, no name at all?"

"Nope. Mom says she ain't got round to it yet, but soon as she thinks of one, she'll let us know. Meantime it's B.B."

"I see," I said slowly, not really understanding at all.

16

How could you have a child and forget to name it? I even named my dolls, all of them. Never forgot one. Well, maybe it would work out for the best, though, 'cause when his mama finally came up with one, it'd really be great. After all, she'd had three years to think of one. Bet she'd do better than Lorraine Harriet.

Noah walked on 'cross the field to his home, but he came back later with friends — Jonatho and Dub, which was short for "W.," which was short for William. Man, these folks even cut up initials! He also brought a little girl named Eleanora, who was called Doby, and a sweet little girl named Doretha whom everybody called Piggy. I would have been quite offended, but she didn't seem to mind a bit. It was amazing how these folks could re-create themselves just by changing their names. We played together that day and became good friends. Every year that I go back, I seek them out for at least one good time.

I finished my fish and walked out to the yard. Since everybody was eating now, it would be the only time that I would be able to steal a few minutes of peace and quiet before the weekend got into full swing. The thick green grass felt like a soggy carpet beneath my bare feet, somewhat disgusting but also kind of refreshing. I was surprised to see Grandpa sitting in his chair under his favorite tree. I'd thought he was resting inside.

"Hey, girl," he said with a slow, weak smile. He never bothered to learn all of our names. I guess thirty-three grandchildren were just too many to remember. He did make note of whom we belonged to, and that was enough.

"You one of Doris Fay's little yellow twins. When did you get here?"

17

" 'Bout an hour ago. They made some fish, you want me to get you some?"

"Nope, already ate."

"What you doing, Grandpa?"

"Talking to my tree."

"Talking to your tree? Does it talk back?" I giggled.

"Nope, that's why I talk to it, 'cause it don't talk back. If I got something in me I need to set free, I don't tell it to nobody 'cause colored folks got loose lips, and you may hear it again, on down the road. But a tree will hold on to all your secrets 'til the Lord comes by and picks 'em on up."

I was about to ask more about this tree business when Cousin Lela walked up and gave Grandpa a big hug. "Do you know who I am?" she asked me, like it was the million-dollar question. Every year at reunion time, grown folks you hadn't seen for a year or more seemed to find great amusement in tormenting you with the game of "Do you know who I am?"

"You're my cousin Lela," I responded quickly. Hah! Couldn't fool me. Score one for the young folks. I remembered one year asking my mother how Cousin Lela was related to us 'cause I couldn't quite follow the blood line. "She isn't actually kin," my mother explained. "Her mama had to go up North to get a job, and she couldn't afford to take Lela along with her, so she brought her to Mama to keep awhile till she got on her feet. It was only supposed to be for a few months, but it wound up being ten years. She was raised up along with the rest of us and we just called her 'Cousin.' Far as we are concerned, she's 'family.' "

"Cousin Lela, they made some fish this morning for

18

breakfast. There's probably some left, if you haven't eaten."

"Actually, I was hoping for one of Bessida's fish and grits breakfasts. I'll be right back, Papa George." Now, if she's Cousin Lela, shouldn't she call him Uncle George? This reunion stuff was one big brain teaser.

"Grandpa, what kind of person was Grandma? I have her name, you know. I'm Lorraine Harriet."

"Your grandma was something else — spit and fire, and a looker, too. First time I saw her, she was visiting her people down this way and she came to our church. Sat right in front of me. She had on this wide straw hat, so big it blocked my whole view. Couldn't even see the preacher, but to be honest, I wasn't listening no way, just kept thinkin' 'bout the girl under the big hat. Hadn't gotten one look at her yet, but she sho' smelled good, like a springtime flower garden. I kept wondering if she was as pretty as she smelled. I knew I would have to wait until after church to really look at her, and I couldn't wait. That was the longest service of my life. When the minister gave that final prayer, I jumped up real fast and moved into the aisle before she could get away. When she finally turned around, she was pretty, just like I thought she'd be. Smooth brown skin, two sweet dimples, and nice white teeth — couldn't stand a woman with a raggedy mouth. She had on a yellow dress, and I noticed that she was a good-sized woman, not one of those little bird women. Nice hips, too, good birthin' hips, and strong arms. I figured she could really move a plow if she had to.

"Yeah, she was my kind of woman. I asked her what her name was, and she said 'Harriet.' Prettiest name I ever heard. I told her mine was George and I was a Snowhill Burney.

"I asked her if I could come by later after supper and swing on the porch with her. She smiled real shy-like and said she guessed that would be all right. I told her to look for me at six o'clock, not a minute after. That evening we sat and just swung back and forth. She took her hat off, and I could see her hair. Made sure it wasn't too nappy. Sometimes a woman wears a hat like that 'cause her hair is all napped up, but not Harriet. She had a nice thick braid, kind of twisted on top some kind of way, and she still smelled good all them hours later. We sat there just swinging, not too much talking, but that was fine.

"I decided right then and there that we made a right fine pair, and if she wasn't spoken for, well, I was speaking up. I told her we ought to get hitched. She seemed right surprised, said if we was going to get married, we ought to wait at least a week. So we waited one week. Planting time was comin' round, and I didn't have a whole lot of time."

"A week, Grandpa? How could you know you were right for each other in a week?"

"What's to know? She was pretty, went to church, came from good folk, and was sweet as pie. She had good plow arms and wide birthing hips. I knew that first night it was right. Waited a week 'cause she wanted to."

"Love at first sight. How romantic."

"I reckon so. We was married for twenty-five years, and I couldn't have asked for better. Gave me ten beautiful children. I was right about them hips. She kept a clean Christian home and worked like a field hand to help me sharecrop enough to get this place. After she died, I never married again 'cause it didn't feel right, no other woman living off what she died to bring about. I asked the doctor what killed her. He just shook his head. I figured same thing that kills so many colored women: she just wore out. Body got tired and just stopped. But she ain't never complained. Ain't never seen none better. Don't reckon I ever will. Harriet, my sweet Harriet."

Later, when Grandpa went into the house to take his nap, I sat in his chair under the tree to see if I would feel any of the magical wisdom that seemed to surround his seat.

"Lorraine Harriet, granddaughter of Harriet Burney." I guess this chair was magical 'cause stuff was even starting to sound different. "Lorraine Harriet," I said it again. Even better. "Well, old tree, I think it's starting to fit. I may wear this name after all."

AFTERTHOUGHTS

"It is through our names that we first place ourselves into the world."
— Ralph Ellison, 1969

Like so much of our history, the right to name ourselves has been a struggle laced with heartache and pain. We have been called Boy, Auntie, Uncle, Nigger, Boot, Colored, Sambo, and Pickaninny. These are but a few of the titles that were bestowed upon us without our consent. From the very beginning of our American existence, whites had the power to call us whatever they wished without reprisal.

During the days of slavery, the master often made the decision as to what our names would be. Even when parent's wishes were apparently different, in the end it was the master's right as property owner that prevailed. Sometimes a slave's name was changed as he or she was sold from plantation to plantation, with the new master having absolutely no regard for the person who stood before him. From time to time, a slave would choose his own nickname, insisting that during private moments only this name was to be used. It was never used openly, and it had no legitimacy, but it was one small and significant act of rebellion that enabled slaves to reclaim themselves for themselves.

When freedom came, the use of only our first names by whites when addressing us was a constant reminder that we didn't merit the same simple respect and courtesies as they did. Sometimes we solved this dilemma by naming our children Lady, Mister, Captain, Sir, or Mayor. It was our way of saying, "Call me by my first name if you so insist, but you will respect me whether you want to or not." The Civil War did finally win us the right to name ourselves. We didn't have much, but now we had that. It was our way of recognizing that "well, we ain't what we ought to be, we ain't what we gonna be, but thank God we ain't what we was." At the turn of the century, we began choosing European names, but we varied the spellings and the pronunciations to make them truly our own. For example, Alvin (European) became Alven, Alvan, or Alvyn, and Alberta (European) could become Albertha.

Dr. Newbell N. Puckett, a college professor, sociologist, and folklorist, has been central to our understanding of African American naming practices. Puckett searched through birth certificates, school records, armed-service rosters, and census data to document some 340,000 names used by blacks. He traced the history of African American names from 1619 to the 1940s, paying particular attention to the names that were the most unusual and that showcased most evidently African American creativity in naming practices. Myself, I don't have to look for the unusual and off-center. I grew up around wonderful folks like Linwood, Alrutheus, Salathia, and Bessida.

In addition to African American names' representing the creative, the humorous, and the sociopolitical thought behind our struggle to establish an identity, our names for our children often paid homage to those African Americans who made us so very proud. We named our children George Washington Carver and Martin Luther King because we recognized greatness and wanted a little bit of it for them. We named our children after the biblical folks because we were always hoping for some of God's saving grace, and we now give our children African names because we are regaining something that was taken from us. I guess that's why I carry the name Lorraine Harriet like a badge of honor. It was meant to be. So if you want to get my attention, then just call me by my name, and you'll know exactly who I am.

Sorrow's Kitchen

"Aunt Bessida Lee. It's me. It's Lorraine, Auntie," I yelled as loud as I could, walking through the front door as if I had already been invited in. No answer.

"Aunt Bess, did you hear me?" I yelled again.

"'Course I heard you," arose a reprimand from behind a closed door. "The whole neighborhood can hear you, the way you screaming. What you trying to do, wake the dead? This ain't New York, you know. Folks don't run around here raisin' a ruckus. Now hush all that fuss and go in the kitchen. I made a peach cobbler. I'll be out directly. What are you doin' here, anyway? Last I heard you was somewhere in Virginia."

I smiled at my scolding. As long as she was fussing, she wasn't ailing too badly. Aunt Bess knew why I was here. She was my mother's oldest sister, and in recent years she had developed kidney trouble. She was on dialysis but still managed to get around a good bit. Still, whenever I was passing through, I stopped in to check on her to make sure

24

she was all right. She had six children of her own, a large church family, and a loving community that were also completely devoted to her, but I didn't feel right if I didn't look in on her myself. She had assured me time and time again that my worrying was for naught, because, as she put it, she was too stubborn to roll over and a mite too busy to die. She and the Lord had it all worked out, and the rest of us looking at her growing feebleness and ever-thinning body just weren't privy to her and God's greater understanding.

Peach cobbler. It wasn't my absolute favorite, but it looked too good to pass up. She must have just made it, because it was warm to the touch and hadn't even been cut yet. Actually, you didn't cut one of Auntie's peach cobblers; you scooped. Underneath the top layer of mouthwatering flaky crust were big hunks of sweetened peaches wallowing in their own juices. I had gained fifteen pounds in recent months and really didn't deserve this treat. With any luck, Aunt Bess wouldn't notice, and we would get through the visit without any unpleasantries.

The bowls were kept in the cupboard, right above the sink — her "everyday dishes." None of them matched, and the designs were faded. The style was also quite dated, but Aunt Bess refused to throw them away, insisting it was foolish to toss perfectly good stuff aside just because you could afford new. As long as they could serve, they could stay. I picked out a pretty one with a floral design; at least it looked as if it had been floral at one time. I scooped a big helping of peach cobbler into the bowl and sat down to eat.

I looked around the kitchen. Everything in its place, as usual. If this kitchen were in a brownstone in Greenwich

Village, it would be called eclectic. Nothing really belonged with anything else, yet all managed to live together quite comfortably. Everything was old and worn but a treasure all its own. The peach cobbler was delicious. Auntie had given me the recipe several times, but it never came out quite right when I made it. Maybe you only get peach cobbler like this if you make it in an eclectic kitchen. I smiled at my own witty humor. *Eclectic.* Aunt Bess wouldn't have any idea what I was talking about — best to keep my wit to myself.

There was a faint scent in the air besides the delicious aroma of peach cobbler. The windows were open, and the spring breeze had already come in and swept most of it away to mingle with the sunny afternoon, yet some of it had stayed behind, lingering leisurely in the . . . oh, yes, I recognized it now. How could I forget that smell, or the memories associated with it?

". . . Ouch! Aunt Bess, that hurts! Must you torture me this way every time we visit? I swear, you must really not want our company if this is the way you insist on treating us when we come to see you."

"Quit that foolish talk, and ain't I told you 'bout swearin'? — it can't be helped. If your mama did what she was supposed to 'fore you got here, we wouldn't have to go through this. She just packs you up and sends you down here, nappy heads and all. You ain't going to church with me with a head that looks like this. Now bend your head and hold down your ear. I got one more little piece here in the back and I'll be 'bout through."

The hot comb would sizzle its way through my resistant

26

locks, determined to bend the stubborn strands. The grease would come in contact with the steam heat and hiss in anger, threatening to pop little hot drops all over my neck and shoulders.

"There is nothing wrong with my hair," I protested. "It is clean and combed. Just because it isn't straightened doesn't mean it's not acceptable. I prefer my hair natural and not altered to fit some white man's standard of beauty." That ought to get her attention. Who could deny the validity of such a sociologically sound argument?

"What's the white man got to do with your head? If the Lord wanted us nappy, he wouldn't have given us the straightening comb. Now be still and hush. Look at your sister: one hour and I was done. Two hours with this head and I ain't made a dent."

"It's a natural, Aunt Bess," I continued. "I go to the barber once a week, and he shapes my hair to fit my face — natural and feminine. This way there's no fuss, no bother. I just wash and go. Besides, a lot of sisters are wearing their hair this way."

"A barber? Ain't never heard tell of such. A woman ain't supposed to visit no barber. I didn't even go inside when I used to take the boys. Why don't you just shop at the men's store and use their toilet, too?"

"Let's just change the subject, Aunt Bess, because you'll never understand. I just wish that you could see what this is really about. My hair makes a statement about me and my dignity. It speaks of pride. It's more than a haircut. I wear my hair natural for the same reason you refused to dye your premature gray. Why didn't you color your hair when you were only sixteen? Now look at it — so beautiful, I couldn't imagine it any other way."

"Gray hair and nappy hair ain't the same. 'Least I look like

the woman God made me. I just don't understand you. I spent
years growing that head, and now it's all gone. You all mixed
up, that's what I say. Young folks, you all just plain crazy. . . ."

I never did get Aunt Bess to understand a great many
things I had to say, despite the fact that I spent years trying. To me, it was understandable, symptomatic of two
black women reared in two different times and two different places. How many of my contemporary sisters have
heard echoes of this same dialogue between them and their
older kin? But misunderstandings should never be allowed
to chip away at the love you have for one another, and for
Aunt Bess and me, they never did.

When the phone call came from my mother, I was expecting it but was in no way prepared for it. "Your aunt Bess
has passed. You need to get ready to travel. The funeral will
be at the homeplace on Saturday."

The funeral was short and sweet. I was determined to
be strong. I was scared that if I let one teardrop fall, there
would be no end to the avalanche of my sobs. When it was
over, I waited until everyone filed out of church and went
to look at Aunt Bess one last time. "She looks like herself,"
Aunt Maribelle had said, as if that were any consolation.
Her gray hair had been brushed so that it was shiny like
silk. It had even been greased, I noticed with a smile, the
first glad feeling on a somber day. Aunt Bess would have
liked that. Somebody had been crazy enough to suggest
that we bury her in a wig because her hair had thinned out
quite a bit at the end. "Never!" I argued. "Her hair was her

crowning glory, and her personal statement deserves its final voice."

I went back to the house. I refused to go to the burial. I didn't think I was up to that. The funeral had been trying enough, and I was holding myself together by fragile, fraying threads of strength. I walked into Aunt Bess's bedroom and checked my face to make sure my makeup was still fresh and my hair was still in place. The short natural really did flatter my face in a way no other style had ever done. I patted down a few runaway strands and was quite pleased with my overall reflection. I even looked presentable by Auntie's standards.

It had been quite some time since I had been in her bedroom. Sparsely decorated with a select few furnishings, it hadn't changed much. I sat down on the bed, something I would never have dared do if she had been alive. The same quilt, the same old nightstand that held the now-ragged family Bible, and the same old rocking chair that had been my grandmother's. Once, in my foolish youth, I had suggested that she get rid of this junk and let us all chip in and buy her some new furniture. Why had I said that?

" 'Junk'!" she screamed as she threw my carelessly tossed label right back in my face. "I will have you know that these are family heirlooms. This Bible has been in our family for five generations. This nightstand was given to me when I first got married, and this here quilt belonged to your great-great-grandmother. Don't you know the story of this quilt?" I knew the story by heart, but I also knew she would welcome the chance to tell it to me once again.

"Why, this quilt is made of precious scraps pieced together by your great-great-grandma's own loving hands. This piece right here is part of the calico dress her sister was wearing the day that she was sold away. Those two sisters vowed they would try to find each other again one day, but in the meantime they never wanted to forget, so they ripped their dresses right then and there and exchanged rags. Years down the road, the slaves were freed, and she hoped that she and her sister would be able to find each other again. This scrap would be like a beacon bringing her loved one home. After a while she reckoned she would have to be content to meet up with her sister at the Lord's pearly gates, but as long as that scrap lasted, her sister would never be forgotten here on Earth. That story's been told a hundred times, but the message ain't never changed and it ain't never lost its meaning. This quilt is over one hundred years old, and it's worth ten of them fancy bedspreads you keep buying me. 'Junk' indeed!"

Aunt Bess taught me a lesson that day that I would not soon forget. I never again made mention of redecorating or replacing her "junk." I guess sometimes we can get a little ahead of ourselves, and folks got to take us back a step and teach us a thing or two, but I pride myself on being a quick study and on never having to be taught the same thing twice.

Everybody would be coming in soon. Better give the kitchen one last look to make sure everything was perfect. The church missionary circle had brought over enough food to feed an army and had it all set out so the family wouldn't have to do a thing. This kitchen, I thought sadly, would never be the same.

Peach cobbler: someone had brought over a big dish. I reached up and pulled down a bowl. I got out a big spoon and was ready to scoop, only this one wasn't made like Auntie's. This one you had to cut. Disappointed, I decided to pass. I heard a car pulling up, and the voices alerted me to an impending intrusion. I was ready to sit down and wait on the others, but it was then that I saw it, just lying there on the stove's front burner. She must have forgotten to put it away the last time, in the wooden cabinet like she always did. The hot comb. It had to be at least ten years old, or maybe older than that. Rusted and corroded, but it still worked, and as long as it could serve, it could stay.

I fingered the teeth on the old hot comb. It still had a few droplets of grease on it, and some silken gray strands. I wrapped it in a napkin and put it in my purse. It was a family heirloom now — another of those ever-present, gentle reminders. Goodbye, Aunt Bess, I whispered as I gave the comb one last shove to make sure it was secure. I reckon I'll see you at the Lord's pearly gates, but in the meantime, I'll make sure you're never forgotten here on Earth.

AFTERTHOUGHTS

The Africans believe that there are three phases of existence: the *living,* the *living dead,* and the *dead and gone.* The first phase, defined as living, is self-explanatory. I hope all of you who are reading this book are in that category; if not, well, I don't want to know about it. The second category needs some clarification. The living dead are those who have moved on to another spiritual place but will not be truly gone from this world so long as there is one person still alive who remembers their voice, can picture their smile, or can tell their story. As long as there is even one person remaining whose life has been touched by that individual in a very personal way, then there is still something left here to hold on to. The last category, the ones who are dead and gone, are the folks who have completely moved on from this world to the next. There are no longer personal connections that exist to link us to them. Their very essence has been completely removed, so that though we can hold on to them through a spiritual understanding, they are quite simply no longer a part of our world.

My aunt, God rest her soul, still has a place in this world if we look at her passing the way the Africans do. I can still hear her voice, visualize her smile, and tell her story, and I do all three every chance I get. My children have no memory of this wonderful woman who played such an important role in my life, but I try to keep her and others just like her as real as I possibly can for them because I want her to touch their lives in the same way that she touched mine. Memories are so important for African Americans because so much of what we know has never been written down — all we have left of some folks is the memories that we've tucked away in our hearts.

The Freedom Garden

The potted plant peeked out over the windowsill to watch the goings-on of the crazy folks on the front porch. I hadn't noticed it before, but the little thing had started to look kind of shabby. Not that it seemed to be doing poorly, mind you, just a few dying leaves round the edges. The plant was just like the haughty old woman who had cherished it to her last — its back was still strong and straight despite a few frailties and some distressingly droopy cleavage. It probably wished that it could speak up and give me a piece of its mind, but today it would have to be content if I got the message that it needed a glass of water. There was no doubt about it, this little plant was one of us. Spunk to the backbone: It was obvious Aunt Clo hadn't left us after all. Only a Burney would have the nerve to make demands while its dignity was hanging raggedly around its knees for all the world to see.

Well, it was clear that my wilting flower needed some fairly immediate tender loving care. All right, I'm coming — no need to start fussing. I could just pick off the few withering blossoms that dangled rather disgracefully from its pitiful little limbs; that might spruce it up a bit. Then after it was looking somewhat presentable, at least decent enough for company, Miss Addie from across the road could tend to it whenever she came by to check up on the house. Now that Grandpa was gone and there was nobody here except on family-reunion weekend, Miss Addie was kind enough to look after things year round. It worked out pretty well, too, because she had nine children, all living at home, so coming over here was probably the only peace and quiet she ever got.

I could just leave her a note if she didn't come by and say hello like she usually did. I looked over at my bleak little bucket beauty. Somehow just giving it a glass of water didn't seem to be enough. After all, it would still be dependent on the kindness of strangers. Maybe I should plant it outside in Grandma's use-to-be garden, and then it could fend for itself. The Lord would provide the essentials, and then this spunky little foliage could take it from there. The downside was that the old garden out back hadn't been looked after for years and years.

I ventured out back and discovered that I was right: the place was a mess. The small family plot that had given so much and asked for so little was now like a gracious old friend who had outlived her usefulness and then been tossed rather carelessly aside. She was still a beauty, though. Her face was aged now and rather weather-beaten, her features worn to almost nothing, but still there remained strength and courage chiseled amid the time-honored old grooves. The long, lush vines, vibrant green leaves, and brightly colored blossoms that used to make up her marvelous crowning glory now lay mangled, tangled, and disheveled in a sidelong heap. Sadly, she looked woefully unkempt. She used to be quite the sassy lady as she ambled throughout this entire place, just strutting about like a proud peacock on patrol, but she was tired now, and unabashedly dragging. Well, it was obvious she wasn't able to take care of herself. She deserved our devotion and desperately needed my attention, but she was too proud to beg, and I really couldn't blame her. She knew we had been raised to do better than this. Grandpa always said that he believed in praising the bridges that helped carry him over, and if I listened carefully, I could still hear him a-talkin' and a-testifyin'.

"Girl, get you some dirt," he told me one day while crawling on his hands and knees, lovingly running his fingers through the damp ebony soil. "Colored folks ain't got too much they can call their own, so the only chance we got for making it is land. Our folks just took off north like there was some promise of a better day, but I've been there and I ain't seen nothing too special. Yeah, they come back driving big cars and spitting first-class, but like I said, I done been there and seen it all for myself. Folks living on top of each other and paying for the privilege of borrowing somebody else's own. They call it rent. I call it foolish! Just give me a little black earth like this here, and that's good enough for me."

"But Grandpa, didn't you ever want more and get angry when you didn't get it?"

"Well, I guess the Lord didn't see fit to give me too much, but I got my soul, a little common sense, too many know-it-all kin, and this here parcel that's all mine. Ain't nobody gonna take it from me, neither, 'cause long as I got it, I can take care of myself. Now sometimes your soul can wander astray, your good sense can go on holiday, and your kin can crowd up on you, squeezing away at your peace and tranquillity — but the land will never let you down. T'ain't really much difference between a good acre and a good woman — you take care of her, and she will take mighty good care of you. This here lady has been taking care of me and mine for many a year. Now, you young folks got it a whole lot better than we did, so you better dig in, grab hold, and make something of yourself — something that will make you grin from the inside out. Then get you a few dollars, put 'em away for a rainy day, and pray the bank don't fall with your money underneath it! But baby, you only gonna pass by this way one time, and sometime in your life, you got to get you somethin' that will be there for you when the going gets rough or the times get tough. Where do you think all them fancy-dancy colored folks gonna end up when the white man decides to take back them few trinkets he give 'em? I'll tell you where: right back here in Dixie, nose to nose with all they tried to run away from. You listen to Grandpa, 'cause I believes in lifting them up that help carry me over, and this woman of mine"— he patted the ground affectionately —"she done loaned me her back on many a dark and cloudy day."

Now, as I cradled the pot, I realized that I had two damsels in distress on my hands. Well, I'd best see to it that Aunt Clo had a spot to lay her weary head, and what better place than nestled in the bosom of an old family friend?

"Oh, look over there, Aunt Clo," I whispered to the

plant. "There's that sweet little whippoorwill again. What a beautiful black bird! His husky little singing voice reminds me of Uncle Earnest lettin' loose on one of his wonderful blues songs. I still remember Uncle's music, even though I haven't heard it since I was a little girl. Listen, Aunt Clo, isn't that just soothing to the soul? You know, a lot of folks believe that when some black people die, their spirit comes back in the way of a whippoorwill, forever searching for home and ever ready to sing their lowly love lyrics for anyone who cares to listen. Do you think that could be true, Aunt Clo? According to Miz Addie 'cross the way, that same little bird comes back to this spot every year at family-reunion time.

"Wouldn't it be wonderful, Aunt Clo, if that bird some-how managed to capture a little piece of Uncle's soul as it was on its way to Heaven? The family was so broken-hearted when he left home. He didn't have much more than two suits, two dollars, and his one stringer, but he was determined to make his way to fame and fortune. To leave like that, during those tough times when every family round here needed every able body workin' just so they could make it, and Uncle Earnest decides to take off — Aunt Leana told him that if he left, he might as well keep going for the rest of his days, because he would never be welcomed home again. I guess he took Aunt Leana to heart, 'cause that's just what he did, and nobody has ever heard from him again.

"Oh, I remember that every once in a while I'd hear Uncle Pete humming one of his little songs, and if I caught him in just the right mood, he'd even teach me the words. Lord, Uncle Earnest was something else, wasn't he?

I got me a song
that sings 'bout the blues in me.
Blues as blue as the deep, deep sea.
Got me a song
that sings 'bout the sorrows of the soul.
Sorrows as dark as a big black hole.
I got me a song, got me a song
And I aim to sing it
yeah sing it,
all this day long.

"You know, Aunt Clo, even if there isn't one shred of truth to that old superstition, I'm going to just believe that over there is Uncle come home again. It's comfortin' to know that despite all the bitterness, in the end, family is family, and it's all that ever matters. Some way or another blood always rises to the top, even if it has to climb over some stubborn obstacles. If my family history is correct, Aunt Leana wasn't the only one whose temperature would rise whenever Uncle Earnest's name was mentioned. I seem to remember you being quite angry at him as well, so I guess that end of the garden is out of the question, or the two of you will take what Grandpa called the beautiful earth beat and turn it into a hot raging rhythm — and I wouldn't want that!

"But where to put you, Aunt Clo? Over by the fence looks like a good place. That's where the vegetable garden used to be, but it's mighty close to the cornfields where all the lovers used to meet — it might offend your Christian sensibilities. It sure is a pretty spot, though, and you'd be near all those wonderful wild herbs; they would surely help your aches and pains. You would also be near the well, and what I used to call that 'patch of mourning glory' 'cause of Aunt Maribelle's habit of sneaking back after a family funeral when she thought none of us was looking, swiping flowers off the gravesites, and replanting them out here. I used to think it was creepy, but now it seems great that everyone who has left us in one way is still here in another — kind of like you. But that means Uncle Joe is over there, and he'll tease and taunt you until you're screaming for a moment's peace, though at least you would never be bored.

"Then there's that spot over there. It's a nice spot. I know it firsthand because when I was ten years old, I went digging for Great-grandma's silver that you said was buried out here somewhere. I was sure that had to be the spot because I noticed for years nothing ever grew there, but unfortunately I came up empty-handed. Boy, that sure is one heck of a story about Great-grandmama Catherine and that silver. Imagine a black woman bold enough to steal away from slavery during the height of the Civil War. Determined to leave thirty years of hardship with more than just the clothes on her back, she sailed right out the door with the white folks' silver. Just tucked that silver underneath her unmentionables and walked right on out the door — and walk she did, over three hundred miles, here to Farmville. Married her a preacher, and much as he hated it, she flaunted that misdeed by using that silver every chance she got. She wouldn't even listen to the church folks who told her that the silver was sinful and that eating from it would tarnish her soul. She told them straight out that she wasn't scared of the Devil or the white folks neither, and as long as her back remained scarred, her skin stayed black, and her life was still hard, then she had a right to eat her collards on the best there was. Spunk to the backbone, Aunt Clo. I tell you, we Burney women are something else.

"Too bad Great-granddaddy wasn't nearly as bold, or we might know where that silver is today. He was so scared that some kind of evil was going to land on them that he would bury that silver after each and every time Great-grandmama used it. Buried it out here for good the day she died, and refused to tell anyone exactly where it was. But it's out here somewhere if all we've been told is true. Maybe you'll get lucky and end up near it. Might as well live large while you can!

"Look over here, Aunt Clo, all them pretty dandelions. This was the spot where the rose bushes used to be. All of them beautiful roses caused quite a stir around here — poor colored folks with the most beautiful flowers in town. Poetic justice, if you ask me. Now there's nothing here but weeds and wildflowers, but Grandpa would say that these are every bit as beautiful as his roses because it's all God's handiwork. I really think this is the perfect spot for you, Aunt Clo."

It didn't take but a moment to dig the shallow hole that was needed for the new dwelling place. The earth was still damp from the morning drizzle, so the soil was cooperative and moved quite easily. "Well, Aunt Clo, you certainly seem pleased with your new surroundings. Nothing like a little sunshine to warm your spine and some fresh air to cool your heels. I should have known — you always were the prissy one in the family."

It was getting dark, time to be getting back. Now which was the best way out? Looking for an easy exit was interesting not only because of all the different pathways that had been etched in over the years but because of all the understandings that were so deeply ingrained there as well. You could see that some folks took the long, scenic way round, others efficiently went through the middle, and some kind of dragged their way through, while others seemed determined to run over everything, stirring up the dust the entire way. But like the spirits that lingered here, each pathway was a testament that neither in living nor in dying was there ever an easy way out. The Burneys were survivors, though, and no matter what, we'd always made our own way.

AFTERTHOUGHTS

The African American garden tradition took hold in the South during slavery and has held its own ever since. Yams, okra, collards, and other plants from West Africa grew in small provisional gardens that slave owners often encouraged and sometimes ignored. For many enslaved Africans, these gardens were the difference between survival and starvation, and their unique African traditions displayed themselves proudly in these cultural landscapes. Sugar cane, ground nuts, and watermelons grew together, usually sharing a rather small plot of land.

This comingling technique was not only distinctive and intriguing in its appearance but also highly effective as a way of cultivating edibles. Mixing different plant types, rather than separating them into neat little rows as the Europeans preferred, seemed to create the necessary "garden climate" for bountiful harvests. Layering plants next to one another according to their different heights apparently reduces the insect population and discourages diseases and weeds by shading them out. This method also efficiently conserves soil nutrients and moisture.

The slave garden was very much a part of the plantation landscape. The enslaved Africans often worked their gardens in their free time and sometimes sold their vegetables at stands along the road or at the town market. Most often, the garden provided much-needed food. The ability to garden and maintain their gardening traditions gave the enslaved some sense of independence and allowed them to retain some small measure of humanity.

Gardening was then, and still remains today, a significant part of the African American experience. Following the harvest, the canning and freezing of fruits and vegetables have become family traditions. Kinship around food is as essential to cultural tradition as it gets.

I have incredibly fond memories of my mother's oldest sister wearing her big hat and dragging her New York–born niece to yet another field to pick the perfect strawberry or in-season butter bean. She was ill, getting more and more feeble, and was fully able to get someone else to do this for her, but that was out of the question. She had to feel the dirt underneath her fingernails and the sun across her back. She had to personally pick the vegetable and place it in her ragged old sack. She didn't know any other way. She loved the land, the beautiful black earth, and she thanked God for the bounty He delivered each and every season. These were blessings pure and simple, goodies that with a little faith and some loving care could be ripe and ready for the taking. There didn't seem to be much joy in the eating if the getting wasn't personal. My aunt, like so many others, took it personally — very personally. My folks, they talk to their plants, whisper wisdoms to trees, and sing to wildflowers. Maybe that special place the land held within their hearts goes beyond just the handpicking of foodstuffs — but goes clear back to Africa, where the belief was that everyone who left this world left a little something of himself or herself behind for Mother Nature to nurture and protect.

This was the purpose and inspiration for "The Freedom Garden," to pay tribute to the land and to my folks in a way my aunt and my granddaddy would have appreciated. Every time I walk past a collard-green patch or a cotton-field, I smile because I know there are some remnants of my people still out there somewhere.

Homefolks

One of the Homegrown Angels

Sister Nellie moved on around the tiny grocery store, making sure she hadn't overlooked anything. She couldn't understand why so many folks liked to shop at the new supermarket way 'cross town. It was so big that all you did was wander around trying to figure out where you just come from and if this was someplace you had just been. After a while, you got so tired and confused that it was all you could do to find the quickest way out. It wasn't till you got all the way home 'fore you realized you ain't got one bit of shopping done. Didn't make no sense, least none that Sister Nellie could see, especially since it was so easy to shop at Jimmy Lee's.

"You got everything you need, Sister Nellie?" asked Jimmy Lee. "Just holler if you need something, you hear?"

"Thanks, but I'm still looking," she said back. The tomatoes didn't look too hot this week. Mister Jimmy Lee must be fussing again with Sister Clara and had to go to Rosa for his tomatoes. Rosa was sweet as she could be, but everybody in Farmville knew she didn't know a thing about vegetables. These were too small and didn't look too juicy. These had to be Rosa's — Nellie would know them anywhere.

"Mister Jimmy, what you and Sister Clara fighting 'bout this week?" she asked. "I thought you two would be married long 'fore now, but the way you two keep feudin', you won't never get that chance to say 'I do.'"

"That's got to be the stubbornest woman the Lord gave to this world," Jimmy Lee answered. "I've tried to marry her, God knows I have. All I did was tell her that I wouldn't mind marrying her, but first there got to be a few changes. . . ."

"'Changes'? What kind of changes?"

"Well, it just don't seem right, me being a man of God and taking up with a woman who smokes a pipe and swigs moonshine. And she don't just swig it, she makes it, too! Every time I go see her, she's got carloads of folks comin' round blowing for her special brew. It ain't right, I tell you. It just ain't settin' well with me, and I can't have all that in a wife."

"I see. What did she say when you explained all this to her?"

"Well, I didn't rightly explain it, now that I think about it, 'least not like I'm explainin' it to you. I kind of lost my head before I got the chance to say too much."

"Lost your head?"

"Yeah. I was so darn mad when I went to courtin' her Saturday and seen them moonshine bottles all lined up there by the door that I just took and hurled every last one of them in the ditch. Boy, was she mad then! Took out that rifle of hers and threatened to fill my britches with buck-shot if I didn't get the heck out of there right then. She said she wasn't going to let no man tell her how to live or what to do! Well, I just got out of there quick as I could. I ain't said one word to her since, and I ain't goin' to. When she sees the error of her ways, she'll be beggin' for my forgive-ness, and then if I decide to take her back, it will be on my say-so. Meantime, well . . . hey, how did you know I was fussin' with Sister Clara? She come by and tell you?" He eyed her suspiciously.

"No, a little bird told me," said Sister Nellie with a grin as she spotted one particularly pitiful tomato.

Just then a young man came in, looked to be about six-teen. Sister Nellie looked him over real good, trying to fig-ure out who he could belong to. He was slope-headed like the Richardsons. Every one of them Richardsons was slope-headed. Folks said the grandma marked 'em by get-ting mad at a neighbor one day and hitting the woman in the head with an iron. The Lord was punishing every last one of 'em for the sins of the past, so they was all born slope-headed. She looked again at the young'un, this time eyeing his knees. Only folks got knees like that would be the Williamsons. Everyone of 'em got skinny legs, big feet, and knock knees. He sure had Williamson legs, but then again, every one of the Williamsons got squinty little eyes like Chinamen. They always look like they're falling asleep when you talk to 'em, and this boy here got big bug eyes like the Waters folks. Bug eyes, every last one of 'em. They all got eyes so big they look like they can see through you and around you at the same time. Poor boy, he got big ears, too, just like the Johnsons. Sister Nellie's daddy always said the Johnsons were so mean, cheap, and stingy they'd steal the grit from your teeth if you let 'em, that's why the Lord give 'em big ears. She wondered who he could be. Didn't recollect seeing him in these parts before.

"Hey, chile, I'm Sister Nellie, and you look mighty familiar, but for the life of me I can't quite place your face. You stay round here, and if you do, where? You got people in these parts, and if so, who? You saved, boy? Have you met the Lord? Do you go to church around here, and if you do, where? I declare, I must know you, 'cause I knows everybody. Well, speak up, son, I can't hear you."

The poor boy was so dumbfounded that all he could do was stand there and stare at her. He didn't know that anybody that old could talk that fast. "I beg your pardon, were you talking to me?" he asked.

"'Course I'm talking to you. Ain't but two of us here, and I sure wasn't talking to them dried-up tomatoes. I ain't gone crazy yet, no matter what them other folks say. Now, you heard me, I want to know who you are, and I don't plan to keep repeating myself, and kindly refer to me as 'ma'am' or 'Sister Nellie.' Ain't you got no respect for old folks?"

"I got plenty of respect for old folks. It's just that I didn't consider you to be old."

Oh, he was a charming devil, Sister Nellie thought. Maybe he was related to the Colemans. Everybody knew that any one of them Coleman boys could charm the underpants off a nun if he had a mind to.

"Sister Nellie, you just caught me by surprise. I'm here from New York, where my mama and I had been living since I was born, but I've got family here somewhere, and

50

that's why I came. My mama died seven months ago, and she told me a little, but not much, of her growing up here. I'm trying to track down as many relatives as I can before I have to get back to school in the fall. That doesn't leave me much time — maybe six weeks."

"Six weeks! Boy, I could find your family back in Africa by then. What was your mama's name? Who was her daddy? Where did she live, and why did she leave? I got to know all that before I can help you, and it's my Christian duty to help you, so that's just what I aim to do."

"Well, now, Sister Nellie, I don't expect that you *can* help me. I mean no disrespect, but this all happened a long time ago, and believe me, I know what I'm doing. I'm going down to the courthouse and search for all the appropriate documents, and then I'm off to the Hall of Records. I took a special family-history course just so I'd be prepared. So, Sister Nellie, I can't expect you to tell me too much with us just standing here."

"Well, I can tell you not to buy those tomatoes, 'cause Sister Rosa ain't growed a decent vegetable in fifty years, *and* I can tell you that you coming home with me so I can fix you a decent meal, 'cause you New York folks don't know spit about cooking good country food. After that, you going to tell me what you know, and I'm going to surprise you by telling you how much I already know. Now get your bag, you coming with me, and if you need tomatoes, get 'em in the can." Sister Nellie picked up her bag and hollered, "Brother Jimmy, we leaving now, I'll see you next week." Then she slipped a brand-new ten-dollar bill on the counter and told the young'un to move it along 'cause it was time to go. Well, what else could he do? She hadn't

51

given him much of a choice, so he paid for the tomatoes and off he went, too.

The kitchen was sort of like Sister Nellie herself — very, very open, a little too warm, and way too country — but he was hungry, so he figured he'd stay.

"You got a name, boy? I would hate to call you 'hey you!' I don't know what you all do up in New York, but it sure ain't the way *I* was raised." Sister Nellie moved fast, too, he noticed. She'd already put away half the groceries, and he hadn't quite made it to the chair to sit down. He noticed that she'd already put a pot of water on to boil. He was in the South now, and he wondered if he shouldn't offer to help. No; on second thought, he'd best just sit.

"Name's Louis, ma'am."

"Got a last name to go with that?"

"Yes, ma'am — Washington, as in Booker T."

"Well, if you can't claim some relation to him, I'd keep that wit to myself, 'lessen you was trying to figure out if I knew who he was. If that be the case, you ain't got to wonder no further. I never met the man, but I know who he is. We do get books down here in the country, leastways every once in a while. Now, was Washington your mama's name or your daddy's?"

"It's my mama's name. I don't know anything about my daddy, ma'am. All I know is my mama left him here when she came north. I don't even have a name to go by, and when I looked at my birth certificate, she conveniently left the space for 'father' blank. On all of her important papers she didn't even name a next of kin, but in the spot that calls for who to contact in an emergency, she put the name Elsie Smith from somewhere down here. I've already asked around, but nobody here knows her. That's really all I got, but I'm smart. I'll find out, even if it takes a couple trips and many, many years."

"Elsie Smith — I don't recollect. Where you staying, by the way, while you doin' all this lookin'?"

"With a friend of mine from New York who has family about twenty miles out in Winterville. I got him to drop me off here in Farmville so I could look around. He'll be back for me about eight." He looked at the pot on the stove. The water should be boiling soon. He wondered what she was making. He was really hungry now.

"You got a picture of your mama, boy?"

"Yes, ma'am." He pulled out his wallet and handed a worn little picture to Sister Nellie. It was in pretty sad shape, but she could make out the face, all right, and Lord have mercy, she knew just who it was. She'd recognize the child anywhere, only this wasn't a child Nellie was looking at, but a mature lady. Sister Nellie wondered if her spirit had grown up like her body had obviously done. She'd like to think that somewhere along the way she'd become a real woman, at least woman enough to make a decent life for herself and this child.

She looked at the young man in front of her and smiled. She handed the picture back to him and mumbled a few words about what a fine-looking woman his mama was. Why hadn't she seen it all before? The boy looked just like him — Mister Henry's son. She closed her eyes. All of a sudden her insides hurt. What now? She ain't never been one to run from anything broke if she could fix it, or from a job to be done if she could finish it. But the Lord had taken this out of her hands. It wasn't her place to say a thing. There really was only one thing to do — step grace-fully out of the way.

"Excuse me one minute, son. I got to go back to make a phone call. I'll just be lickety-split." Sister Nellie won-dered if he had seen in her face that she knew something she couldn't say. Her daddy was always saying her eyes couldn't hide a thing. But the Lord had spoken; this just wasn't hers, and she would be respectful and stay in her rightful place.

She made her call and came back quietly in the room, so quietly he didn't even hear her return. He wondered what was happening. What had she seen in that picture that had been too much to share? Maybe if he was patient and gave her a moment, she'd tell him what he desperately needed to know.

"Anything wrong, ma'am?"

Wrong? Oh, it was all so wrong, baby, she silently thought. You probably the only right thing come out of it. She remembered everything — after all, it hadn't really been that long ago, maybe sixteen or seventeen years ago that Rosa had taken that girl into her home when she had nowhere else to go. Gave her a mama when she needed one most, and loved her like she was one of her own. And what did Rosa get for all that? Nothin' but hurt. Came in from the cornfields early one day and found that child and Mister Henry in the barn spread 'cross the hay, lovin' each other as bold as you please. Rosa threw her right out the door, and shortly thereafter, she threw Mister Henry out, too. It took him two years, but Mister Henry finally wormed his way back into Rosa's good graces and then back into their home. They seemed to have found their way back to each other by the time he died ten years later. Anything wrong? Lord, son, more than you know, but I've already called Rosa, and angel that she is, she told me to bring you on over. This was Rosa's own now — if not by blood, then by an unspoken and inherited responsibility. Rosa would do right; she always did.

"Ain't nothing wrong, son. I called a friend of mine who may be able to help you out, that's all. I told you a little bit 'bout her back there in Mister Jimmy's store. She said to bring you right over, so we got to head out once again. Now pick up your tongue, boy, she did say something 'bout dinner. Gumbo, I do believe."

Sister Nellie climbed up on the counter, opened the top cabinet, and started looking. Frightened that she might fall, Louis begged her to get down.

"Hush, child, I ain't that feeble, that old, or that unsteady. I been climbin' this counter thirty years, and I ain't fell yet. Here we go. They right here, I thought I had some," she said, and handed him three cans. "You hold on to the vegetables. If we going to Rosa's, we gonna need 'em. She sure is sweet, but she and vegetables just ain't on one accord."

Minutes later, Sister Nellie and Louis were on their way. She looked at him again. He really was a fine young man. She hoped he'd find all he was looking for and then some. "Well, Nellie girl," she whispered to herself, "you done stirred up the stuff, let's just hope it don't stink."

"You say something, Sister Nellie, ma'am?"

"Not a thing, boy, not one blessed thing."

AFTERTHOUGHTS

Whenever I tell stories about mamas, I always remind folks, in my own poetic way, exactly who it is that I'm talking about. After all, in the African American community there aren't just mothers, there are also mamas. Mothers raise their own children. Mamas, on the other hand, raise everybody's children. So I rarely tell stories about mothers, but I sure love to tell stories about mamas. They are a part of a cultural tradition of loving that should never be forgotten. Lord, how I love my mamas!

The aunties, the sisters, the grannies and the nannies,
the missus, the mamas, the madams, and the mammies,
the bloodmothers, the other mothers, and the ones we called
    ma'dear.
All those ladies who lived in grace
with their spitfire spirits and souls of sweet lace,
who could saunter down Decent Street, still swing their hips,
dab a drop of vaseline, and shine their lips,
and when they rouged their cheeks of sweet honey brown
they shimmered like a rainbow 'cross a muddied ground.
They never knew that they made all the difference in a cold
    cruel world,
with their hot-combed locks and paper-bag curls. . . .
But Lord bless 'em and keep 'em, every last one of 'em
'cause without them where would we be?

I think that of all the stories in this book and the multitude of folks presented here, my favorite story to write was "A Homegrown Angel" and my favorite character to create was Sister Nellie. I took her right out of that legacy of women who knew that being a mama could take you to the schoolhouse, the courthouse, or even the jailhouse. You could leave out the front door and not even know where you were headed, only that you had to go on. As long as there was one child suffering, there was room on your lap, a place in your heart, and some more mothering to do. All of those timeless beauties with their now-wrinkled cheeks and withering wombs who in all of their wisdom still knew how to love and taught the world how to mother — what a wonderful legacy they have left to each and every one of us.

I have succeeded in becoming a mother — the birthing of my four children took care of that — but I am constantly striving to remember also to be a mama. Maybe that's why I became a storyteller: I believed it would allow me to touch children in a very special way. When I tell them a story, it's like grabbing hold of them, pulling them right into my lap, and wrapping my arms around them. For just a little while, all can be right with the world, and I can take them to special places where folks still love one another and a dream can still come true. Unfortunately, the story has to end, and that group of children ultimately must move on, but the blessing is that there is always another group coming along that will also need a mama. When they do, I'll be ready for them.

God bless Sister Nellie, with her homemade loving and wonderful homegrown wisdom. Yes, Lord, bless and protect the Sister Nellies everywhere. Amen.

Gettin' Ready

If Emma Jean James had bothered to take a real good look at all that the full-length mirror was flashin' back at her, instead of tryin' so hard to reach on round to pat herself squarely on the back, she would have realized quick that she looked 'bout silly as silly could be. But Emma Jean James wasn't payin' no mind to the sinfully snug blouse, the too-tight tan skirt, or the shoes that looked to be at least two sizes too small. If Miz Nellie had been there, she sho' 'nough would have told her that it was just plain foolish to try to shove ten pounds of lard into a five-pound bag. But Miz Nellie was nowhere to be seen, so the only thing Emma Jean had to think on was how special she was 'cause she was the very first colored to work for the First Farm Insurance Company.

True, Old Man Hess had been given a position at the company sometime last year, but he'd died 'fore he could even get started good — so that didn't count. Emma Jean James, though, was young and ready to go. She had sat through the entire two-week training course and received her very own clipboard just yesterday. Why, Emma Jean had an even better job than that know-it-all Catherine Cook, who had gone clear to Greensboro and gotten to go to college for almost two years. Now look at Catherine — Emma Jean thought — doin' nothin' more than slavin' in her mama's kitchen, up to her elbows in flour and grease, bakin' bread that went for a dime a loaf or a penny per slice. Emma Jean James wouldn't be caught doin' nothin' like that there. No way; only the best would do, and now she was an agent for the First Farm Insurance Agency.

The first house on the list was Miz Lowe's. She owed two dollars on her burial policy, and she had to pay today or be cut off. She had been payin' kinda regular — 'least up to last month. The company might not have known it, but Emma Jean suspected Miz Lowe was havin' a bit of hardship 'cause she had taken sick last month, and had to go twice to see Doc Walker. He charged at least a dollar a visit. Emma Jean knew 'cause he had taken care of her recently when she split up her big toe.

"Watch out for that Miz Lowe," Mister Brown at the insurance company had warned. "She'll pull out that Bible in a minute, and by the time she's through preachin' and prayin', she done bought her a whole 'nother month free of charge. She's a sly one, that Miz Lowe," he said, "but sly or no, I know you'll be able to handle her just fine — yes, I reckon you'll be just fine." And she would be, too. Didn't her mama always tell her that she was the smartest of all her kids? Mister Brown would be at the office today at five o'clock sharp to get her report and pick up the collection.

She only had a few houses today, so that would give her plenty of time to do what she needed to do.

Miz Lowe's house was on the corner of First and Bell End. It was in pretty sad shape, too, now that Mister Lowe was gone. He'd been dead for a while now, burned up in that factory on Castle Hill what used to make them pretty candles. Yeah, this was the right place, but how was she supposed to get up all these steps? These here were rotted clear through the middle, though they seemed sturdy enough on the outer edges. Normally she would have just spread her legs the width of the steps and climbed her way up real careful-like, but today, in this skirt, that wasn't even a possibility. Emma Jean looked on around her — there was nobody in sight, nobody who would see, so it would be all right. She lifted her leg, held on to the rail, and hopped herself clear on up to Miz Lowe's front door.

It took a good deal of knocking to summon Miz Lowe, but Emma Jean knew she was in there, and she wasn't 'bout to give up easy. Miz Lowe looked out and gave a raggedy li'l smile. Emma Jean remembered how she used to have two gold teeth where her front ones were supposed to be, but when the hard times hit, she'd knocked 'em out and sold 'em just to keep herself going. Didn't even go to Doc Walker so he could pull 'em proper — just went to Mister Bell's shop with her mouth still bloody and asked him straight out what she could get for 'em.

"Hey there, Miz Lowe. How you doin'? I don't know if you know it or not, but I'm the new girl for the First Farm Insurance Company. Got me a name tag, a clipboard, and everything. Now, it say right here that you owes two dollars on that burial policy that you got, and I come to get it. It also say that you gots to pay or else. . . ."

"Or else what? Ain't but one Jesus, and that's the oniliest one that I bow down to. Come on in and rest your feet. I got some iced tea made. Girl, you sho' done got big! How's your mama? I ain't seen her in a month of Sundays." Emma Jean knew it would be a mistake to follow Miz Lowe into that parlor and then sit herself on one of them dusty old Victorian chairs with the smelly velvet and threadbare seats, but she did it anyway. She had two dollars to collect, and if one glass of tea was the price to pay, so be it.

The tea was pretty good, and the glass did appear to be clean, so Emma Jean figured she could afford to relax a li'l. It was obvious Miz Lowe was in a pretty good mood, so maybe this wouldn't be too tough after all. She sat back and took a deep breath. As the musty smell of mildew and dirt pervaded her senses, she realized relaxin' might be a terrible mistake — best not to get too comfortable. It was really time to be gettin' on her way. She was just about to speak up when she noticed that Miz Lowe had grabbed hold of that tattered li'l Bible of hers that was settin' on the coffee table when they came in. Uh-oh, trouble!

"Miz Lowe, that tea was good, and it sho' was nice of you to be inviting me in, but I got some stops to make 'fore I got to be at the office early this evenin'. If you would just pay that . . ."

"You know your Bible, girl?" Miz Lowe cut in. "I know you go to that new church they built 'cross Big Road, and I don't claim to know what that young preacher is teachin',

61

but mine tell me you got to live by the word. You eat a piece of this here," and she lifted her Bible accordingly, "and you ain't never got to be hungry."

"Yes, ma'am. I know, ma'am. My mama done raised us up with a righteous hand — she say all the time that our house been anointed with the power of the Lord. Yes, ma'am, my mama has done her Christian best by all of us, but today I ain't come to talk about the Word. I come to —"

"I know why you come. The Lord told me all about it last night, but I can't be dealin' with the ways of the world till I tend to my Father's flock. Now us old sheep already know the road, but you young lambs, well, you still got to find your way. I got a message for you, girl, and I aims to deliver it."

"But Miz Lowe —"

"Hush up, girl. You ain't supposed to be talkin' when a saint is in the spirit. Now I was lookin' here at Matthew," and she turned to it in her Bible, "and there's a story in here that you need to know somethin' 'bout. You see there was this humble servant, sorta like you — you servin' them white folks what got that insurance company, ain't you? No, don't answer that, 'cause I already know you are 'cause you told me that when I first opened the door. Anyway, like I was sayin', this servant come to his master and beg him to forgive all his debts, to have just a li'l bit of mercy. Well, the master forgive him like he was supposed to, and the servant went on his way. Later, that servant come up on a fellow that owed him some money, and do you think he forgive *him?* No siree, he commence to tryin' to beat the money out of him. He clean forgot what the other had done for him. You see how easy peoples forget what they ain't want to remember? Well, folks heard 'bout it sho' 'nough and went back and told that master that forgived him. Well, that master was mighty put out by how that servant was actin' — shameful, just shameful. It's a disgrace what some folks do in this world.

"Now, you take them two dollars I owe. I ain't got it now — won't have it till next week — but I ain't worried 'cause you a good girl, and you remembers how I took care of y'all when your mama wasn't able. It wasn't easy for me, but I'm steady on my feet when I'm marchin' for the Savior. I reckon that's been 'bout ten years ago. I know you remembers it, 'cause I sho' do. Like I said, I ain't worried 'cause you a real good girl. Don't let that Devil walk on side you, you hear? Cast him to the wind. You tell that company of yours you got to see me next week. Now go on, chile, and git. You got a job to do, and you won't have it long if you don't git to it. Oh, and tell your mama I said hey."

Emma Jean figured this second stop ought to go a li'l bit easier. It was Miz Lucille's house, and she always had plenty of money. Nobody had ever told her exactly what Miz Lucille did to get all that money, but where she got it from wasn't none of Emma Jean's business anyway. Miz Lucille owed a dollar on her account book, and she was gonna get that dollar or her name wasn't Emma Jean James.

"Hey, Miz Lucille," Emma Jean said when Miz Lucille came to the door. "Right pretty day today, ain't it? I'm the new girl at the First Farm Insurance Company. This here is my first day. See here on the name tag — it say *Agent*. That's me, Agent. I come by to get that dollar you owe, and then I'll be on my way."

"I can' believe them crackers hired no colored! How you get a job like that?"

"I guess I'm just smart. Them white folks like clean coloreds, and the ones who's smart, too. Yeah, I reckon that was what it was. I's just smart. It's a real good job, too, and I aim to keep it. My mama's so proud — you ought to see her, she's grinnin' from ear to ear."

"Well I got yo' money, you ain't need to be worryin' 'bout that. I did a funeral Wednesday past and made two whole dollars. I put aside one 'cause I knew this bill was due."

"I don't understand, Miz Lucille. You workin' for Joyners or somethin'? Ain't nobody told me that."

"No, I ain't workin' for no Joyners. What I mean is I'm a cryin' woman. I just did that big funeral in Wilson, and I did the best job I ever done. Woman told me to cry good and loud but not to get snotty or slobberin'. Told me if I could get the whole place goin' good, there would be somethin' extra in it for me. Well, I knew what to do. I waited till they played 'Amazin' Grace.' They dragged it good and slow, too. I waited a minute or two and then I let my tears just rip! Started out with a nice soft boohoo and worked my way to wailin' in no time flat. In five minutes I had the place all tore up. Everybody was goin' then. I looked over at that woman what asked me to come, and she seemed real pleased. I made two dollars for that one — usually I just get a dollar. Wasn't you at Deacon Easeley's buryin'?"

"Yes, ma'am, I was."

"You don't remember how I carried on? Took me near 'bout twenty minutes to get them folks going. I thought I'd run out of tears 'fore I got 'em going good. Just when I was 'bout ready to forget it, Old Lady Mae Rae jumped up and hollered. Once she went, all the others followed right after. I only got half a dollar for that one 'cause the Widow Easeley is my friend. Some of that sadness was for real."

"You mean you get paid to put on like you're grievin' and moanin' over the dead, just so other folks get all riled up?" Emma Jean couldn't believe you could make a living like that.

"'Course I do. That's too much work to be doin' for free. You got to have you a little bit of spirit in a place if you want the dead to leave easy. Don't nobody die round here 'less I got a say in things. Onliest time I ain't got nothin' — well, they offered, but I wouldn't take it — was for that Thompson boy who died two years back. You remember him?"

"Yeah, I sho' do."

"Mama got tired of bein' a mama and took that young'un and strung him up in the middle of a cottonfield. Just lynched him like he was a thievin' Georgia nigger. My soul bled for that one there, and the tears that fell, well, I give 'em freely. Seem like my heart 'bout stopped at the buryin'. Sometimes I wonder 'bout folks like that, headin' straight to hell in a handbasket. Here, you take this dollar, and be sure to post it to my name. Don't put it next to nobody else's. I worked hard for that dollar, and I don't want nobody else gettin' the credit. I reckon I'll see you next month unless you goin' to Miz Patricia's funeral. You goin'?"

"Yes, ma'am."

"Oh, have I got something special for her! Mister Allen probably gonna want to pay me a dollar and a half. I got this moan all worked out, sound like it's comin' straight from the gut. Then I shut my eyes and add this li'l rock that I got, swayin' my body from side to side. The moan gonna start slow and easy, kinda soft-like, and then it's gonna get louder and louder. I figure it won't take but ten minutes to heat that whole place up. I didn't care too much for Miz Patricia, but for a dollar and a half, I'll cry for Satan. You go on, now. I'll see you Wednesday at the buryin'."

Mister Joseph's house was nestled among a forest of briars and weeds. It was in town, but as she approached the two-room cabin, Emma Jean couldn't help but feel like both Mister Joseph and his humble dwelling would be more at home in a Carolina tobacco field. Mister Joseph looked to be 'bout seventy, but nobody knew for sure 'cause Mister Joseph himself didn't even know. He told everybody that his mama had died early on, and after she passed, didn't nobody seem to take care of his age.

He had never married. Instead, he'd spent most of his life tendin' and takin' care of old Mister Frank, who had been gone now for over ten years. Mister Joseph was in front of the house now, steady tryin' to piece together what was left of a fence that should have been torn down long ago. Today, instead of steppin' high and movin' lively, he looked like his tiredness was comin' down hard on him.

Emma Jean looked down at her clipboard. Mister Joseph owed five whole dollars on his insurance. He was such a sweet man — a li'l strange, but that just made him interesting. Nita Bay always said that he might be one of them hants that rides around disturbin' good folks, 'cause one time she seen him when mosquitoes was buzzin' all around him. They had been pretty fierce that day 'cause it had been rainin' for three days before. Well, while everybody was busy swattin' and poppin' the best they could, old Mister Joseph wasn't put out in the least — and soon Nita Bay figured out why. Every time a mosquito would land on him and bite, it would just fall off dead. She seen it with her own eyes. Now, if Mister Joseph wasn't some kind of hant, then how come he could kill them mosquitoes like that? But none of that was anything Emma Jean needed to know. Only thing she had to worry on was gettin' that five dollars and puttin' it in the book. Lord, she hoped he had it. This job wasn't as easy as she thought it'd be.

"Hey, Mister Joseph," Emma Jean yelled loud as she could.

"Hey yourself. What you doin' round here?"

"I'm the new agent for the First Farm Insurance Company. See, I got a name tag and everything. I come by to get what you owe. It says here that it's five dollars. I can just get that and then be on my way."

"Five dollars, huh? Well, that ain't no surprise. It's been five dollars a month since I can remember. I took out a big policy — so big the white folks worried I wouldn't be able to keep it up good, but I ain't never missed payin' up."

"Mister Joseph," Emma Jean said, "I don't mean to be

steppin' 'cross no lines, but I can't help but be a little curious. You ain't got no family, Mister Joseph, and your policy is so big. You don't need near that much for somebody to put you away decent. Fact is, you could be buried for free at the Friends of the Sinner Cemetery since you ain't got no church home — 'least I don't think you do. Who gonna get all this money? You ain't got no outside kids don't nobody know nothin' 'bout, do you? I mean, like I said, I don't want to be steppin' in your stuff, especially since you elder and all. But you a nice man, Mister Joseph, a right nice man. I just don't want you sufferin' no hardship on account of this money — this five whole dollars every month! That's a lot of money. 'Course the First Farm Insurance Company would be 'bout ready to give me the boot if they heard this here, but they ain't got to know. I sho' hate to see you spend that money if you don't got to."

"I'm leavin that money to Ebenezer Baptist Church. They ain't know it yet, but they will when the time come."

"You a member there, Mister Joseph? I been to that church, and I don't recollect ever seeing you."

"I ain't no member, that's true. I ain't a member nowhere. I'm leavin' that money on account of Bishop Tucker what used to be the pastor there. When my mama died, I ain't had no one. I wasn't more than six summers in age, I figure, but 'course I can't be too sure. Well, when my mama ceased, I couldn't think of nothin' else to do, so I run out the house and went and hid in a ditch over yonder. I stayed there and prayed for God to bring my mama back. Old Bishop must've followed my footsteps there, though at the time he told me Jesus led him straight to me.

He was a good man, too — real good. When I raised up to be a li'l older, he tried to get me to join his church. Wanted to baptize me proper and point me in the direction I needed to go, but I wouldn't let him."

"How come, Mister Joseph? How come you ain't let him?"

"'Cause at that time I just ain't had nothin' for no religion. Never did forgive God for not hearin' my prayers 'bout my mama all them years back. It's too late to get with it now 'cause I ain't got no faith or no experience. I ain't sung them songs, I ain't prayed them prayers, and I ain't read one word in that Good Book. When I did think 'bout joinin' twenty years back or so, old Mister Frank told me there wasn't nothin' to all that religious stuff 'cept the ruination of some good livin' here on Earth. I figured if there was a Heaven, it ought to be a place people wanted to go, but I reckon I won't ever know. I think my time is almost up here — dreamed of that white horse, so I know it won't be too long.

"I don't remember much 'bout my mama, but I know she was a faithful woman. But that old Mister Frank, he didn't go too strong for none of that there. Wouldn't let nobody talk 'bout Jesus and such. All them that worked for him, 'specially the coloreds, were sho' 'nough kept in the dark. Didn't let us read, didn't let us know, didn't let us ask. Whatever it was we needed to get, he fed to us in his very own spoon. He say there was nothin' to all that churchin', and he was a right smart man, so I figured he ought to know. I guess even the learned can be wrong 'bout some things, and old Mister Frank might've cost me more than I thought. Sometimes, though, when my spirit sinks low, I shut my eyes and I try to pray, but don't nothin' come but more emptiness."

Mister Joseph was lookin' off into the distance, and Emma Jean was choked up with sorrow. He reached in his pocket and pulled out five dollars. "Here you go, you take this. Maybe it will buy me some of your God's good grace. Buryin' insurance and faith — I reckon you need a li'l bit of each, just in case. Yessiree, just in case."

AFTERTHOUGHTS

They sang spirituals about the glory of leaving one world and moving on to the next. They formed societies, even in the midst of slavery days, to ensure that someone would look after the "gone on." They defied their masters and snuck out into the night, gathered together, and laid loved ones to rest. They sometimes waited in cemeteries to see if the dead did indeed sing and shout around midnight. They told awesome ghost stories, and they believed them. They decorated gravesites with personal artifacts so the deceased would feel at home, and when they couldn't afford a traditional marker, they used their creativity and made one like no other. They superstitiously believed such truths as, "If a person dies without speaking his or her mind about important matters, he or she will purge" — that is, foam at the mouth after death — "until it is all out." They buried their dead from east to west like they did in Africa, and they celebrated passings with food, music, and fellowship. The African American burial tradition is a rich legacy with three hundred years of strong history behind it.

Booker T. Washington once said about his own people, "The trouble with us is that we are always preparing to die. You meet a white man early in the morning and ask him what he's preparing to do — he is going to start a business. You ask a colored man — he is preparing to die."

I'm not quite sure I agree with that statement completely, but I do know there is some truth there. I acknowledge that in the days when Mr. Washington made this statement, it was probably more realistic to plan to die than it was to start a business, if you were colored, anyway; but be that as it may, the reality is that for African Americans, death has always been one of the most important moments of life.

The Africans have always believed that you show your love for someone by providing the best you can upon his or her death. The status and worth of a man were measured by the way he laid his people to rest. That heartfelt conviction — the urge to do one's best for the dear departed — traveled across the seas and landed here squarely on American soil. If they were helpless to provide for their kin during life, they would do their best for them upon their death. The spirit of the burial was not a sad one, as many might expect, but a joyous one that brought people together so that they could reminisce and share fellowship over wonderful food. The understanding was that the deceased was going on to a better place than anywhere here on Earth. The place of resting was sacred and significant, and often there were two cemeteries, one for homefolks and kinfolks and another one for strangers and the unwelcomed. The purity of the burial place was paramount, and integrity had to be maintained.

71

The intensity with which African Americans prepare to die is brought truly close to home for me when I remember events and stories involving my own family members. I remember my mother's telling me that my grandfather, during the most financially difficult time of his life, bought not one burial plot but two! And when my mother escaped the cottonfields and headed off to college, Granddaddy didn't have a college fund to help her. She would have to make do with his love and his prayers, he said, but if anything ever happened, he did have a burial plot for her. Thankfully, she never had to worry about that. And if someone in the family died and had nowhere else to go, Granddaddy was always prepared because he had his own plot and then, too, he kept a spare — just in case. My mama reminds me that she wants to come back home to rest in eternity, and I promise I'll do my best by her. That is the ultimate expression of love where my people are concerned: "putting them away proper." If you do that, then folks won't have a thing to say. No sir, not one thing.

Three Sixes

Everybody, anywhere near here, knew about the curse
that Miz Bella spit on the ground, of what now makes up
   Harper Town.
All the folks say that Old Massa Ben Avery,
back in them days of what they called slavery,
took Miz Bella's number-six boy and sold him way, way, way
over thattaway.
Anybody can tell you 'bout how after freedom come,
Old Massa Avery tried to make up for the wrong that he had
   done.
Even the white folks — 'specially them that's way up in the
   years —
still love to tell it, you know the one —
'bout Mister Ben, and them six miles of land what runs
under the sun.
The colored folks here can still hold dear
to that story of Miz Bella, and that land, the land
that soaked up her tears.

They say she stood right there, and spit six times all over
this entire place,
and then threw Mister Avery's land right back in his face.
She told him straight out — least that's what they say —
that couldn't no dirt, no rock, or even no stone
make up for a boy already done gone.
But beware, she told 'em, this mama and this boy number six,
gonna stir up some evil in one hell of a fix.
Well, it was soon after, that some coloreds and some crackers,
   too,
came straight on up here, and they say,
"Mister Ben, we'll take care of that land that soaked up them
   tears,"
and Lord they worked it, too, some say from sunup to sun-
   down,
but not a blessing would grow here
'cause of them three sixes that done come down
right down on this town. . . .

If that white woman that come here from the state relief
office had asked what she was supposed to ask, and done
what she needed to do, she woulda knowed 'bout them
three sixes, and what hell they was raisin' in this here town.
She'd a knowed that Old Brother Mack can't even raise a
hymn in them fields he got there, and I'd a told her that
Sudie and Shug ain't never had no regular work, or steady
money to speak of, but they each done raised a household
of folks, with nothin' more than a strong back, and a worn-
out washpot. If she'd a just asked Miz Jane, not how many
young'uns she'd birthed but how many she needed to feed,

she'd a knowed that Miz Jane got her four *and* them three her sister Bess left at her door.

Yeah, if that Miz R. D. Jones had bothered to walk past them rotted old oaks and strolled a ways behind them trees, she'd a seen that indeed, old Miz Fay do live there, and that tilting old shack is a lot more than a place ready to tumble right where it's at. If white folks were *askin'* folks instead of *tellin'* folks, they would find out all they needed to know. But sad to say, it don't look like it's gonna ever be so.

Now, Miz R. D. Jones wasn't the first cracker to grin that too-wide grin and come round here with a know-it-all cap stuck high on her head. No siree, we had another one I remember, not too long back — Miz Stevens. She had on a white lace dress and dainty little white shoes. She wouldn't even get out of the car good — just peeked out at us and shook her carefully curled head.

She ain't come alone, though. She brought this high-steppin' colored woman with her. She was from up north somewhere. I could tell by the way she talked through her nose and tried to purse her lips when she spoke. Well, it don't matter to me where you come from, colored is colored, even if you tryin' to pretend that it ain't. She was a funny one, too. Pretended like she ain't never seen no hardworkin' niggers bent over a field, tryin to pick out a livin', or ever sat on no stump in the front of the house, eatin' a real sweet watermelon, funnin', sunnin', and spittin' seeds at one another. No, she acted like she ain't know nothin' 'bout that there. And then when I offered her some of my best beans with a good helpin' of fatback, she said she couldn't, on account of they would upset her stomach. How your belly gonna be upset when it's good and full? Don't make no sense to me, no sense at all. No, that woman there didn't know she wasn't no more than one of us dusted off and dressed up. She sho' didn't do us one bit of good, neither. She gave the church a few dollars on account of that white woman telling her to. Then she left 'fore we could really tell her one thing. Sometimes I think folks just like to ask, but they ain't really want to know.

I tried to tell that white minister that come through here 'bout them three sixes what come down on this town. He nodded his head up and down like he was understandin', but I know he still ain't got it. I can tell you that 'cause all he did was tell us to ignore that nonsense and go on about praisin' the Lord, but I told him like I tell anybody else who really want to know — pretendin' that there ain't no hell don't put the fire out. That's what we need, a way to cast that devil on out of here, but I reckon it ain't never gonna happen after Miz Bella's done spit that evil all over this place. It would take one of her own to lift it, and the only one we got that's left of her babies say he ain't never gonna let us forget.

Some of us say that we gonna leave, gonna go somewhere where the blessings are free, and the livin' is easy, but so far we ain't done it. Sometimes I think Miz Bella reaches up from the very bottom of hell and holds us here. Seem like no matter what, we just can't seem to get going, no matter what we do. But we gonna pay the price now, 'cause things around here sho' is pretty tough, and some of us just ain't gonna make it. 'Course if they hadda delivered that promised relief, well, at least we woulda had a fighting chance, but now I just don't know. Miz R. D. Jones been here once, but she ain't never come back, and I don't reckon we'll ever see her or her kind again. It looks like it's just us up against them three sixes, and Lord, they sho' done come down hard, so very hard, on this here town.

AFTERTHOUGHTS

African American folk history came to be when folks looked at the world around them and then wove together story, myth, religious beliefs, and personal experiences. This was an attempt to make sense of some things we can all see but somehow or another still can't seem to explain. In folk history, the historian is one of the folks themselves — some old, some wise, but all talking over the incidents of their lives. If we listen carefully, we can truly begin to understand people and their place within the world as they envision it. They will tell us all we need to know about the cultural, social, and political dynamics moving within their reality. From them, we can also learn the truth about relationships, which is absolutely crucial to understanding anyone: the relationship between the individual and the community, the individual and the family, and one individual and another. Unlike so much of traditional historical scholarship, truth here comes not from artifacts and documents but instead directly from the people who lived it and had the good sense to tell it. The people are the history *makers* as well as the history *tellers*.

This story begins with people talking and telling tales the way all history and literature was passed on before there was formal writing. The talk is folk talk, full of half truths, shrewd meanings, and sly humor. The story has the sincerity of honest folks who believe all they are telling but aren't naive enough to tell all they know. These are folks whose survival has depended on their ability to lower their eyes, but who can still manage to see it all. They have been taught by the elders the art of evasion and irony, as the safe meeting place that lies somewhere between complete, humiliating submission and foolish confrontation. These elders teach an age-old game that is essential to peaceful coexistence.

For me, the greatest part of my work as a cultural historian comes when I am seated at the feet of the elders. It is then that I can hear *our* story in our own voices. These stories are not filtered through a European interpretation that has somehow managed to remove the heart and soul of who we are and where we've been in its woefully inadequate translation of our past. I am not only looking for facts, but also searching for that little bit of mother's wit, the inspired eloquence and wisdom that make the past lively, significant, and personal. As one woman I interviewed so beautifully stated, "Baby, I'm telling you about what I done seen for myself, not something I done heard about or something somebody else done lied about. I'm saying just them things that I personally knows." Well, ya'll, that's good enough for me. Enough said.

Every Other Tuesday Off

Although she was poor, country, colored, and certainly not married to Mister Lonnie Smith, who was Southern, white, and rich, she was still expected to tend to him, cook for him, and lie with him whenever he wished — just 'cause he paid her four dollars a week and called her his live-in. The actual Missus Smith, a snooty white witch, told anyone and everyone who would listen that she couldn't be bothered with no man, least of all the man that was her husband. Still, it was Missus Smith and Missus Smith alone that benefited from a liaison with the bothersome Mister Smith. Missus Smith got the jewels, the house, and easy livin', while all that the long-suffering domestic ever received was abuse, hard work, and lots and lots of heartache.

She looked at the clock — it was near 'bout five. She'd been workin' this kitchen all day long, and her tiredness was comin' down mighty hard on her. There were sure to be at least several more difficult hours added to an already

79

too-long afternoon. Mister Smith was due to be walkin'
into the kitchen any minute now, feelin' quite entitled to
grabbin' him a handful of anything he wanted (unfortunately, that something or another more often than not
turned out to be a handful of her) before he sat down
and waited to be served by the ever-toiling and better-
be-available pretty li'l colored woman. She dreaded the
evenin' to come. Soon as that fool was full, he would be
ready — ready for her. He would grin a real big grin (like
the Lord done poured ridicule all over his face) and then
he would wait for her to grin one, too. She never did,
though — the best she could ever manage was grittin' together her teeth 'bout hard as she could muster, and then
reluctantly swallowing back the hateful words that threatened at any moment to spill 'cross her lips. Their coupling
was way too wretched, and far too regular, to suit her,
but it seemed to be big fun for the old man, Mister Smith.
At least three times a week he would make his way to the
drafty li'l back room 'cross from the kitchen to graciously
gift her with the use of his body (thank God his generosity
never lasted for more than ten minutes) 'fore he stumbled
his way back up the stairs to lie with his back to the totally
unconcerned and completely uninterested Missus Smith.

Ten years ago she'd had to suffer the attentions of this
same fool, and she'd left when she thought she wouldn't be
able to stand it for a moment longer. But then she'd come
back, and here she was, despite all the promises she'd
made to herself that she would never see this place
again — she was right back where she'd started from because, sadly, she'd had nowhere else to go. She could suf-

fer the tiresome Mister Smith a li'l longer if necessary, 'cause she'd be putting out his annoying li'l fire any time now. Yes indeed, any time now.

That same poor, country, and colored woman now walked slowly through the field that she proudly called her own. Like a death bell, it called her back to this brilliant piece of place, demanding once again that she connect herself to its deadly potential. The burial ground that lay not more than fifty feet away, with its somber markings and bleak li'l squares, honorably held its near and dear, its dead and gone, in grimness and desolation. Here, however, in her own li'l meadow, murder mockingly camouflaged itself in a bed of colorful splendor. Bitter, boastful beauty cleverly charmed the unsuspecting and unknowing into its delicate and despicable clutches.

She stopped suddenly and reached for one of the more ghastly li'l wildflowers. That familiar and sinister bit of glee began to creep through her senses, kinda like one of them real good drunks from Miss Clara's homebrew. She stroked the long, lethal stem and caressed the creepy long leaves. What joy! The fall poisons were back in bloom once again. She plucked one of the pretty li'l flowers and rubbed it against her black cheek. So beautiful. So useful. So deadly. Of course, they had died their necessary annual death; Mother Nature demanded that much of them, but like a ghost who returns to her past, so, too, these li'l blossoms returned year after year to the world of the living, ever flaunting their gruesome glory. Dried, crumbled, and consumed, just a tad could render a fully grown man sluggish and eventually unconscious. Add a bit more and that same man would fall to his knees trembling and salivating like a wild dog. Then, after suffering incredible pain and nausea, he was sure to die an agonizing death.

The tansy plants were right next to the fall poisons. They were tall, strong, and wonderfully scented. Most people saw the clusters of yellow flowers and deep dark-green leaves only as delightful decoration, but when crushed, they exuded the most aromatic of fragrances, and used correctly, they could rid a woman of an unwanted and soon-to-be-born li'l baby, or swell a man's stomach to the point where he would sure 'nough beg to die.

She couldn't leave without a walk to the chinaberry tree. This one was smaller than most but potent all the same. Its large leaves and purple li'l flowers made it absolutely breathtaking to behold. This one yielded the beautiful li'l fruits that begged to be tasted, but just a mere few ingested would leave you stumbling, confused, and paralyzed right before killing you slowly. She picked a handful of leaves and put them in her pocket along with the fall poisons and the tansy pieces. The poppy was looking particularly strong and plentiful, she noticed. She would need just a bit to make sure the dyin' wasn't too painful; she was not without mercy, after all. She would allow him those first few moments of pleasure that this plant could provide — right before she finished him off completely. She had been giving him just enough to get him addicted for quite some time now. He was hooked and didn't even know it. Whenever she wanted to have a li'l fun, she would hold back his much-needed dose and watch him squirm. This evening she would be kind — no more squirming, just instant and glorious death.

The funeral for Mister Lonnie Smith was short, sweet, and to the point. Since he would be joining his illustrious relatives (more Southern and too-rich-for-their-own-good white folks) who had been previously laid to rest in the eternal gardens — the ones that faced the back of the house — the service was held in the main parlor. Missus Smith made an admirable display of grief, weeping just enough tears, and managing just enough moans, to convince a few, if not most, that she was truly sorry that Mister Smith was indeed gone. Maybe, just maybe, she really would miss him a bit. You got to figure that if anything's been next to you for thirty years or more, even if it's been no more than a pain in the neck, surely there will be some emptiness once it's no longer there.

She was the only colored woman in the room, yet she felt completely at ease. She was impeccably dressed in a starched black uniform with a pretty white apron and an elegant li'l hat perched just so on her carefully combed head. The contrast of the white hat against her dark and shiny face made her skin seem even more deeply ebony. She knew her place, and she was good at her job, so this day was supposed to be 'bout easy as easy could be.

She balanced a large silver tray in each hand, both filled to capacity with the fancy li'l foodstuffs that for some odd reason white folks seemed to love to eat. Now, if this had been a sendoff done by her own people, there would be long tables filled with fried chicken, potato salad, collard greens, cornbread, and gallons of iced tea. People would be hugging and laughing, really enjoying the chance to catch up on each others' lives. There would be memories, smiles, and promises to keep in touch. Sorrows from the thoughts of a loved one's leaving this world would be quickly replaced by the realization that for Southern colored folks, anywhere had to be better than here.

As she made her way to the front of the parlor, she stole a glance at the dear departed. He didn't look to be settin' on his high horse now, that was for sure. He looked more like what he had proved himself to be — a pitiful li'l man who deserved to pay dearly for the ruination of one perfectly good colored woman. She had growed up in the white folks' yard, so she knew 'em better than most. You just couldn't keep wrestlin' with them suckers 'cause they would sho' 'nough wear you out. Best way to stop 'em was to put 'em away. She looked at him again — an evil li'l soul cloaked in greedy, sagging flesh. Pitiful. Just pitiful. Maybe she should offer up a prayer for his wicked, wicked heart, and maybe one for hers as well. Nope, on second thought, there really wasn't any point to that. He hadn't been worth talkin' to when he was here, and he certainly wasn't worth talkin' after now that he was gone. Her mama always said there wasn't no sense in singin' spirituals to an already dead mule, and her mama had never lied.

It was raining today, a sure sign that the Lord intended to wash all the traces of the deceased from the face of the Earth. Just to be sure, she would salt down the house to be certain that his tortured spirit never, ever returned to bother her. She was smart enough to know that many a maligned soul would return to the place of its untimely demise. She had taken all the necessary precautions, though, so that neither he nor anybody else for that matter would suspect her role in the passing on and finally the immobilization of one Mister Lonnie Smith. She had removed the tainted evening salad laced with the poisonous stems, seeds, and petals. She had waited until he suffered on through to his last breath, and then once she was sure he was really gone, she had called down Missus Smith, who had in turn summoned old Doc Burke. Doc Burke had done just what she'd figured he'd do. He concluded that Mister Smith's stomach had given out, and it looked as if that "matter of time" had finally come.

She moved quickly and served the last of the food. They were getting ready to move the body to its final restin' place, and she wanted to be sure to give Missus Smith the special something she had for the marker. She opened the kitchen closet, and there it was, a beautiful wreath made by her very own hands. She had picked some special blossoms and leaves from her field just two nights ago. It would just have to rest with Mister Smith — it was only right, after all, since it did contain the very greenery that was sending him to where he was fixin' to go. She smiled. It felt good, too. She was finally shed of him. Good riddance! Well, at least one white devil was down, but there seemed to be so many more to go. A colored woman just didn't seem to stand half a chance 'long as one of them was anywhere round. But they would all get theirs one day, and soon. She was sure of it. Yeah, sure as sure could be.

AFTERTHOUGHTS

The work choices for the southern black woman of the depression era were limited indeed — housework or field work. In my research I have spent countless hours with women now up in age, listening to them recount experiences connected with both. Field work was backbreaking, and a necessity. A sharecropper's spouse and many others remembered plowing from sunup to sundown and then facing an evening of household chores. "Chile," one of my ladies said, "I worked harder than any mule I ever seen and it's a wonder I'm even alive today to tell it."

Working as a domestic had its own ups and downs. If you slept in, you did have a roof over your head and three meals a day — but if you had a family, this also meant you rarely saw your own children, were completely disconnected from your community or any kind of normal relationship with your husband. You were also vulnerable to some white man's unwanted attentions and some white woman's reluctance to put a stop to her husband's illicit behavior.

If you did day work, you had the benefit of being able to bring the leftovers home to supplement the family's usually meager meals, but returning home each evening inevitably meant you were responsible for all that went on there, so work became a never-ending cycle that killed many a woman way before her time.

My sympathy for these women is deep and profound. I have been blessed with both choice and opportunity and it is largely due to these women and their sacrifices that African Americans today have either. Their story is so significant that I just had to include their experience in my book. I decided to take a humorous approach and play a wonderful game of "what if." It gave me a chance to take what must have been a fantasy of many — killing their oppressor — and make it a reality. Let's see: What if a woman worked as a domestic? What if there was some white man there who decided she was there for the taking and some silly white woman who saw it all but decided to do nothing? What if this black woman just eliminated him with no more thought than you give to taking out the trash? How would she do it? Could she get away with it? What if? What if? What if? "Every Other Tuesday Off" is the whimsical answer to those questions.

Women and Men Folks

Hitched

I looked right next to me
She looked so fine
I said thank you Lord
'cause she's all mine. . . .

The bride was shaking, the groom was sweating, the mamas were sniffing, and the daddies were grinning. Now if only the preacher would get on with it, but everybody knew Reverend Joyner wasn't one to be rushed. He had been doing the Lord's work the same exact way for fifty years or more, and it didn't look like he was fixin' to change up now. Somebody said it took him so long to christen a baby girl once that she grew up before he was finished, so he had to marry her instead!

The two witnesses standing up front shifted for what seemed like the hundredth time since this all had begun. Cousin Martha had even started coughing again. She always said that the Reverend's ceremonies brought out her asthma "'cause he always sucked up all the air." Sister Lilla was ushering today, but even she had kicked off both her high-heel shoes, even though she had a great big hole in her left stocking toe! I guess you can't worry about being shamed when you're standing round in a whole lot of pain. Why in the world had she worn high heels on a day like today, a day when Reverend Joyner had been told he could have his own way?

Sister Dora couldn't have been happier. This was a preacher who did his job the way the Lord meant for somebody to join up his folks. Married 'em like he meant for it to stick. Maybe if more of 'em got married like this they'd be together for more than just the ceremony. He sho' was telling 'em, and telling 'em just right. Looked like this was one marriage gonna stay stuck together tight. You know, every once in a while, you tell yourself that this time you ain't gonna say one word 'cause so much of what you already shared ain't even been heard. You done decided that you ain't gonna tell 'em one more thing 'cause they probably wouldn't listen no way, but not Reverend Joyner — he sure is having him quite a say. He's telling it to 'em just like he's supposed to, just like the Lord would have him do.

Sister Joyner knew better than anyone how her husband liked to have his word or two. She smiled as she remembered their wedding forty-nine years ago. The poor preacher had barely been able to get a word in edgewise. When the Reverend asked, "Do you . . . ," her husband couldn't just say, "I do." No, he had to have him a telling or two.

"Do I? 'Course I do. Just look at her, pretty as she can be, and I mean to keep her that way, too. Gonna do more than just cherish her, gonna lift her spirits clear up to the Lord and Savior. Yessirree, we gonna stay together and pray together, too! Do I? You bet your sweet britches I do!"

Next year would be their fiftieth. Everybody said they ought to do something kind of special. Maybe she could even wear a new dress this time, something frilly, pretty, and really kind of fine. Oh goodness, he was clearing his throat and looking right at her. Probably figured out she hadn't been listening no way. Better start paying attention, or sure enough she'd hear about it later in the day. She smiled to herself, thinking that if they did do something special next year, it would be quite a sight to see. That man standing up there would sho' 'nough demand his due. Why, he'd probably want to be the bride, the groom, and the preacher man, too!

"Now, I told y'all I wasn't one to be hurried. When the Lord gives me a message, I ain't got no choice but to deliver it. So y'all listen up 'cause this here ain't only for these two young folks. Some of you out there actin' worse toward each other than Satan loves sin. You sleep next to each other every blessed night and wake up fussin', cussin', and carryin' on again and again. And do you know what gets to me the most? Y'all think that don't nobody know. We ain't blind. We can all see. I can tell you, if you keeps on lightin' into somebody it ain't gonna be long 'fore you got yourself a full-blown fire. Now, you can smother the flames, but I ask you, how you gonna hide the smoke? I know some of y'all ain't heard one word I done had to say, and I ain't even gonna bother worryin' on y'all that is too hardheaded to hear or too far gone to help. I learned a long time ago that it just don't do one bit of good to sing spirituals to an already dead mule. But those of you who still got half a shot at some saving grace, you study on this —

God is good, and he'll give you somebody to love if you let 'em.

"Now, you can make it through the storms, but you got to have sense enough to come in out of the rain. Folks tell me I'm country, but country don't mean stupid! I got sense enough to know that each place got its own beauty, and I ain't never wished for greener pastures 'cause I was happy the Lord gave me all that I got, and when you happy you ain't got to start disturbin' stuff lookin' round for something that might not even be. In other words, you got to figure that love is like them cottonfields right out that front door. Before you give up plantin' your own little patch and start lookin' for somewhere new to lay down your hoe, you'd best to take a second look at your own couple of rows. The Lord done give you the land, now it's up to you what grows, but be careful what you lays there 'cause you gonna reap what you sow!

"Now, folks will tell you that love is blind. It ain't really, just 'cause we think it ought to be — and you'll wish it was if you stay married long enough. But the key to a happy marriage is makin' yourself turn a blind eye to some things 'cause a lot of it ain't that important no way. We start speakin' up when what we need to do is hush up! Why do we always think we got to have a word, a little something to say?

"Well, young man, I hope you been listenin' 'cause I got to ask if you plan on taking this woman to be your wife on this blessed and holy day?"

"I do."

"Now, when you say 'I do' — that yes, you gonna take her — do you really means it? Look at her, son, so young

94

and fine. It's your job to make sure she stays that way, too, not burdened with a whole lot of trouble that gonna make her old and tired way 'fore her time. Then you gonna start mistreatin' her and you'll have some real problems 'fore long. Lift her up, son, even if you got to carry her every once in a while, but if you try and drag her down, well, then you gonna fall, too. And don't always tell her what ain't, but tell her what she does to make you happy in your home and in your heart. Love her, boy, that's all she really wants, and you take it from me, there ain't no better place to start. So when you says 'I do,' you makes sure you means it 'cause the Lord is always lookin', and I am, too!

"Young woman, do you take this man to be your wedded husband, to have and to hold from this day forward?"

"I do."

"Now, remember when you say 'I do,' make sure you means it. Love 'em and keep 'em and remember that when you got a good man, a really fine man, there's always gonna be some she-devil that got her eye on 'em. But if you treat that man good, that's as far as she ever gonna get with 'em. If things get to be where they ain't supposed to be, you won't have to go to no *Black Herald* to find out — you'll be the first to know, and won't nobody have to tell you one thing.

"Hey, who here got ahold of the rings?"

Well, the mamas sniffed louder and the daddies grinned wider. The groom's hand shook so as he tried to put the ring on her finger — or maybe it was her hand that was shaking so — that they could barely get the ring on there. It was a beautiful ring, too, not just a plain gold band like most, but one with little diamonds clear way round. He looked so proud. Just look what he did, he done gave her the finest ring in this here town!

"Boy, where you get a ring like that?" The Reverend was sweating now. He even had to take out his handkerchief and wipe 'cross his brow. "Now, you ain't into nothin' shady, is you, 'cause I ain't gonna have no parts in nothin' that justice ain't askin' righteous to do!"

"No, sir, I saved for two years to get this ring, that's how much I loves her. I wanted her to have the very best."

"Now, son, don't you worry 'bout her *wearin'* the best, you make sure you *are* the best, and the Lord will take care of the rest. Now where was I?

" 'Dark and stormy may come the weather
I done brought this man and woman together
Let none except the one that makes our heart
Pull this here man and woman apart
I therefore declare you 'fore the same
Live righteous, go 'long, and hold up your good name.
You have taken a real big step, now walk side by side
But she's all yours now, son, you done got you a bride!'
Well, the knot had been tied
and this was it.
Lord, they was in for it now
But at last they was hitched!"

AFTERTHOUGHTS

The preacher is undoubtedly one of the most respected members of the African American community, and probably one of our most targeted for a good-natured ribbing now and again. The preacher tale is one of the most popular in African American oral traditions, and these tales are as likely to come from the preacher himself as from a member of his congregation. African Americans like their preachers to be humorous in addition to being insightful, philosophical, and religious. More often than not, a sermon will begin with a funny anecdote, a joke, or a side-splitting story. It lightens things up a bit and puts folks in a good mood to properly receive the message.

My own father is a minister. He is also one of the funniest men you could ever meet. He makes me laugh as much as he makes me think. Even his sermon titles are funny; I remember one in particular that tickled my fancy for a good while, called "What in Hell Do You Want?" A little risqué for some institutions, but in the African American church, it was yet another clever and effective turn of phrase that jolted people to a necessary reality. Some would say that the preacher in "Hitched" is a gross exaggeration; others would claim that they know someone just like him. What's your take on the Reverend Joyner? I would love to know!

Sophie with the Gold Tooth

Oh, chile, I'm so glad you dropped in, 'cause I could use me some company. This here town is a right funny place. I been livin' here my whole life and I figure I understand it better than most, but that ain't sayin too much. Folks round here are the tricky sort, leastways they think so. They steady running all around trying to hide all they sins, figuring on just pushing them through the cracks of living like ain't nobody gonna know, but the heavens got vision far and wide and thank God, so do I. There's a whole lot of folks that would try to do me in if I didn't stay one step ahead of 'em.

I'm gonna poison you
I'm gonna get you
I'm sick and tired of the things you do
I think I'll sprinkle some real evil stuff right round your head
and when the daylight comes, you gonna be dead. . . .

Poor Sister Purlie, just laying there as dead and gone as yesterday's good time. So young, too, I'll bet she wasn't a day over sixty. I knew she wasn't going to be here long. I knew it last week. Took one look at her and she seemed to be wasting away for no good reason at all. I been sick so much till I can tell when it ain't natural. I tried to tell her, I declare I did. I told her someone done put something on her just as sure as I was standing there. I even offered to take her to see Doctor Bug. I knew he could fix her right up, but she wouldn't hear of it. Even tried to warn her 'bout that no-good husband of hers. Never did care for him, and I know these things and then some. Now he's over at the funeral parlor and you can hear his great carrying-on's way over here, but he ain't fooling me. I'm the seventh daughter of a seventh daughter, and I was born with not one caul over my face, but two. I even knows who the witches are in this here town, but they don't know that I know.

Now, you take Brother Jim. He was married to a witch who went riding on her broomstick every night, and he didn't even know it. Well, Brother Jim never was too smart to begin with, but even he started to figure something was wrong 'fore too long. Once he woke up in the middle of the night and she wasn't even there! So the next day he comes over and talks to me 'cause he knows I know 'bout these things and then some.

"Sister Sophie," he says, "when a man wakes up in the middle of the night and reaches over to where his wife is supposed to be and she ain't there, wouldn't you figure something was wrong?"

"Well," I told him, "yes sirree, something is wrong."

"What you figure is wrong?" Brother Jim asked me.

"That's what you got to find out," I told him. Then I told him when he went to bed that night not to close both his eyes, just to shut the eye closest to his wife and watch and see what she did.

Right around midnight his wife looked over at him, thinking he was sleeping, and got outta bed right ready to do her dirt. Just then there was a tap at the window. She jumped up, shed her skin in the corner, grabbed her broomstick, and flew out the window straight to that other witch what was waiting for her outside. Well, at dawn she come riding through the window, flew over to that same corner, and said, "Skin, skin, let me in," and her skin jumped right back on her. Then she crawled back into bed and looked at Brother Jim to see if he was still sleeping. Well, she figured he was 'cause the one eye she could see was shut.

Brother Jim didn't know what to make of all this, so he came back to me. Well, I told him straight out he was married to a hant. Well, he 'bout jumped outta *his* skin. "A hant?" he asked me. "Yessirree," I told him. Well, he didn't quite believe it, so I told him again. "Yessirree, a hant, a witch — she-devils that ride innocent folks and animals while they sleeping. Right round midnight they goes out hunting they prey, and if you ain't careful, Brother Jim, why, she'll get you, too!"

Well, I tell you Brother Jim started screeching like somebody done shot him clear outta musket, but I had to tell him. It was the only Christian thing to do. "Brother Jim," I said, "if you wakes up one of these days in a sweat and your bones is aching you like you a worn-out plow-mule, then you'll know it's her. If you see animals all tied up in knots, then she's been bothering them, too. They rides everything and everybody, don't make no never mind who. A witch can make your cow go dry, and sometimes they even smother the righteous in they sleep! She'll keep bothering you, too, if you don't do what you needs to do!"

Well, I had his attention then 'cause he stopped acting the fool long enough to ask me what he got to do, so I told him. You see, if you wants to get rid of a witch, then you gots to get you a broomstick and put it 'cross your front door. She'll be so busy riding it, she won't be able to bother you. The other thing you can do is put a Bible under your pillow, 'cause she'll have to read every word in it 'fore she can bother you. But really there ain't but one way to get rid of a hant once and for all. You gots to sprinkle salt inside of that skin she takes off, 'cause it will burn her butt if she tries to put it back on. Then she'll just have to leave the same way she come.

I figure Brother Jim must have done something, though he ain't never told me what, but I do know that I ain't seen her no more after that. He got hisself another wife soon after, and they looked 'bout as happy as happy could be. But everybody ain't blessed as Brother Jim. Some folks just can't get rid of evil when it comes on around, and they sure don't always get no second chance at lovin'.

Now, you take me. I had one of them no-good men. He wasn't happy just being a dog at home, he had to go sniffing all over town. Finally he got him one of those shameless hussies that's always after somebody else's man. Not too long after that, I started getting sicker and sicker. I knew then that them two had put something on me, but they couldn't get me like they wanted 'cause I'm always protected. I carries my High John the Conqueror root wherever I go, and I gots my lucky hand in my shoe. Well, soon as I knew what was happening, I went to see Doctor Bug. It might've took all my spare change, but if anybody could do what I needed him to do, it was Doctor Bug. In no time at all he done pulled that evil off me and had it thrown right back on 'em. Then for good measure, I got me a pair of my husband's old drawers and cut 'em in just the right places like Doctor Bug told me to. I cut them really crucial parts to bits. I figure he might have gone off with that no-good hussy without so much as a backwards glance, but I done fixed 'em. I'll bet they ain't having such a good time now.

You can't tell me nothing I don't already know about conjure. I done seen it all. It's gotten so in this here town you can't trust nobody 'cause you don't know who is who, or what is what. I tell you I gots to stay one step ahead of 'em or Lord knows where I would be. Now I'm gonna tell you a thing or two that can help you 'cause that's just the kind of person I am.

- *You can sprinkle salt and pepper around somebody's head and it will sho' 'nough bust they brains out.*
- *If you want to get rid of somebody, then you got to get you some graveyard dirt; the best kind is what's deep down in the grave. Sprinkle it round the door of the person you want gone, and they can't stay after that.*
- *If you want to drive a person crazy, then take a strand of their hair and nail it to a tree.*

102

- *The best tip for a woman is this: The easiest way to hold on to a man is to get a little piece of his clothing and keep it. He can't get away as long as you keep that little rag.*
- *If I starts out and got to turn back, I know it's bad luck 'less I makes a cross and spits on it.*
- *I don't borrow or lend salt 'cause that's bad luck, too.*
- *And lastly, I don't never sing 'fore breakfast 'cause sure as I'm living, I'll be crying 'fore dinner.*

You see, the Lord gave the colored man all the signs 'cause He knows it's the only way we can make it. If my right eye jumps then it's good luck, and if my left eye jumps then it's bad news, and my left eye 'bout jumped out of my head just 'fore Hattie came and told me 'bout Purlie. Poor Sister Purlie, if she'd only listened. You got to do all you can to keep evil away.

Yeah, evil is all around us and it's probably them devilish spirits that got me feelin' so poorly. That's why I didn't go to the service. My sister come by and checked up on me. Then she tried to take me to Pitt County Hospital but ain't no doctor ever meant me one bit of good, so I went to see Bertha the medicine woman instead. She fixed me right up. Now, some folks don't trust her 'cause they figure with the stuff she know, and the things she do, she got to be some kind of witch herself, but I don't believe it. I heard tell that if a woman ain't never been with a man, then she can't be no witch. It's having them connections that hooks her up to the evil. Now, Bertha may have her a fine healin' hand, but Lord, that chile got a face that would scare the backside off a mule! Ain't no man want none of that what she got, trust me. I knows 'bout these things and then some, but like I said, she did fix me right up. Gave me some honey and lemon in a whiskey tea to help me with this cold, and then gave me some salt water for my fever. I been taking garlic cloves for my blood pressure and they seem to be doing me pretty good. Later, I'll take me a swig of kerosene and sugar to kill the rest of these here germs. Sister Bertha did tell me to stand on my head to get rid of this headache, but old as I is, if I stood on my head, I'd have more problems than just a headache!

Poor Sister Purlie, I declare I don't know how we gonna get through the year without her. Who's gonna cook pig's feet for New Year's? And February is the church's anniversary — who we gonna get to lead the choir? I tell you Purlie had a dip and a swish in her marching step that was sinful to just watch. Then in spring, Purlie would always pitch in and help Bertha deliver all them beautiful babies — the result of all that summer lovin'.

I guess we just some good-loving, good-timing kind of folks in these parts, and didn't nobody like a frolic better than Purlie. Right smack in the heart of summer, the whole town comes out for a pig pickin', and nobody makes 'tater salad like Purlie. 'Course I knows her secret — she adds just a little bit of sugar, and a dash of red vinegar right 'fore she mixes it all up. I told you, don't nothing get past me! Oh Lord, and what about the fall? I just don't rightly know how them leaves out there gonna turn without good old Purlie to guide 'em. And then there's October corn shucking. To be so old-actin' and always complainin', Purlie could outshuck the best of 'em. I remember one year after we finished with the corn, we gathered together all them leftover shucks, got us some hay and some scraps we found here and there, and made us some brooms. We sold 'em for ten cents apiece and used all that extra money to get us each a new pair of stockings. Fanciest stockings I ever had! Come that Sunday we was stepping so high that no one could tell us a dat-blame thing.

I figure it's gonna be toughest at Christmas. That was Purlie's favorite time of year. Right 'fore Christmas is Kooner time round here. The men always gets together and makes 'em a drum with an old barrel and a piece of ox hide. Then they gets themselves the jawbone of a mule with teeth still in it, and makes 'em up a one-stringer. Old Man Sam plays the water jug, and me and Purlie could really drag on 'cross a washboard. We would all play and them others would sing loud as loud could be. There did come a time or two when we sounded pretty good, but most times we sounded like a passel of animals caught in a trap — we sho' had a good time, though, so didn't nobody seem to mind. Jimbo always dressed up like the Kooner man. He gets hisself all decked out in all the rags he can find and then puts him on a big buckskin hat that sits so high on his head that he looks like he's 'bout seven feet tall. He comes around dancin' and carryin' on, and all the while he's steady collectin' them pennies. Everybody round here saves up all the coins they can just so they can have them a little somethin' to throw at the Kooner man. Soon as Jimbo's cup gets full, here comes the Reverend with his hand out beggin' for the blessing. I declare God done fixed it so that that man can smell every spare dime.

Well, I suppose that time will march on the way it always

has. The seasons will come and the seasons will go, and eventually one day will just seem to fade on into another. I figure that's just the Lord's doing, and we sho' can't get in the way. There will be joy and there will be sorrow, and those of us who are still here to see it all will be thankful for the extra time, but glory, I just can't figure how we'll move these old lives along without our dear friend. Oh Purlie, baby, I sho' will miss you.

AFTERTHOUGHTS

Superstitions continue to exist and even flourish around the world, including within most technological societies. Many regard them as a throwback to ancient times when humans sought to explain the world around them without facts or appropriate data. Others attribute superstitions to plain foolishness and fear.

The enslaved Africans may have converted to Christianity in large numbers, but they held on firmly all the while to their supernatural beliefs. Complementing Christian faith in the slave quarters was *conjure*, a sophisticated combination of herbal remedy and magical ritual. African Americans believed that illness and misfortune had both natural and supernatural causes, and they didn't want to take any chances on either. Skeptical about traditional white man's medicine, they consulted voodoo doctors and mixed up herbs in small pouches tied carefully around their necks. These little "goofer bags" held everything from dried frogs' bones to graveyard dust, depending on the need and circumstance.

Today, the array of African American wives' tales, warnings, and folk cures is abundant indeed. Travel from place to place throughout the South and you'll find there are even variations and contradictions on common themes. In Alabama you may hear that rain in an open grave is a sure sign that the dead person is heading to Heaven; talk to a North Carolinian, though, and he or she will tell you that rain is a sure sign that the Lord is trying to remove all traces of the deceased from the face of the Earth. There is no consensus except for the fact that the rain is a sure sign that means *something*.

The hant is one of my favorite folk characters. Europeans fear the witch, but African Americans are terrified of the hant. She has the eeriness of the European witch, but with a few differences: the hant is a woman who moves normally throughout the community during the day and then sheds her skin in the evening and terrorizes man and beast alike during the midnight hours. She slips through keyholes and under door cracks, and she sneaks into your room and "rides you till you 'bout smother."

The hant is really more mischievous than dangerous, but to keep her away there are some things you can do. You can keep a Bible underneath your pillow or a broom across your door. There are stories about the victims of a hant taking matters into their own hands. One man claims that when a hant came around to annoy him in the middle of the night, he pulled out a baseball bat and started swinging. The next day, his neighbor showed up at his door with bruises covering the majority of her upper body. He knew then who was the hant, and joyfully spread the word throughout the community.

My mama tells me to flush my hair down the toilet instead of throwing it away in the trash. "The birds may get to it in the trash," she warns me, "and if they do, they'll run you crazy."

This is from a highly educated woman who taught for thirty years. It doesn't make sense — most of her folk wisdoms don't — but it doesn't hurt anybody, either. So I figure, why not? I'll do it just in case. You never know. You just never know.

Miz Lullabel, the Devil, and the Sunday Hat

Now, I don't want y'all to think that I just set around telling tales. I try my best not to get into other folks' stuff, and I work like the dickens to keep folks out of mine. You know it ain't everybody that you can confidence. But I got to tell you something that you really ought to know — a third person in your business ain't never gonna do you one bit of good. Look what happened to them Judsons when Miz Lullabel got through with them. You mean you ain't heard that story? My auntie told me this years ago, and whenever them troublemaking, do-nothing-for-nobody folks come along, I remember this story so I'll know what to do with them.

On down thisaway, there lived an old woman named Miz Lullabel Lee. There really ain't no describing her; let's just say that she was something else. Well, one day she was setting on the porch, rocking back and forth as easy as the summer afternoon, when all of a sudden the Devil came riding down the road on his horse. He stopped in front of Miz Lullabel's house, climbed down off his horse, and started to boohoo like a baby. This tickled Miz Lullabel Lee. She came on round, peeked on down at him, and started grinning like a spooked cat.

"What's wrong with you, Devil?" she asked him. "I would have thought that with as much hell as you've been raising around here lately, you'd be feeling pretty good."

"Well," the Devil said, "it's them Judsons down the road. No matter what I do, they just keep living and loving like I ain't even here."

Miz Lullabel was real tickled then, and she laughed out loud. "Devil, I do declare," she said, "you don't know what you're doing, do you? If you wanted cussing and fussing, you should have come to me. Why, it would scare the horns off your head if I told you about some of the confusion I done started right here in this town. So if you got a hankering for some trouble, you leave it to me."

Now, the Devil figured that maybe he ought to stop weeping long enough to take a good look at Miz Lullabel Lee. She was still laughing hard, but there was a dangerous shine in her eyes.

"Well, Miz Lullabel Lee," the Devil said, "I'll make you a deal. If you can do what I ain't been able to do, I'll bring you a brand-new hat to wear to church on Sunday."

Miz Lullabel Lee was excited now! "A new hat," she said, "like the one they got on Main Street — a big, pretty one with a flower at the top that you tie under your chin. Devil," she said, "you got yourself a deal."

The next day Miz Lullabel Lee went walking down the

road. The first person she come to was Miz Judson out in the yard tending to her flowers and minding her own business. Miz Lullabel Lee walked right up to her and hugged her. Now, how was that sweet woman supposed to know that Miz Lullabel was up to no good?

"I declare, Sister Judson, I ain't seen you in a month of Sundays," Miz Lullabel Lee said. "I woke up this morning and realized that I ain't been real neighborly lately, so I decided to stop by and see you and that mister of yours. How y'all been doing lately?"

"Same as we have been for the last fifty years," said Miz Judson. "That man ain't changed at all. Now, marriage got its ups and downs, but I ain't seen nothing better to replace it with, so I'll just hang with it." Then Miz Judson smiled that real pretty smile that everybody loved her for.

"You know, Sister Judson, it seem to me like I might be able to help you. You know, my mama was one of the smartest women this country has ever seen, the Lord rest her soul. However, she didn't take all that wisdom to the grave with her — she left some of it right here with me. You know we got to help each other, and I believe that I got a little something that will fix you right up." Miz Lullabel's words sounded right interesting to Miz Judson, and she couldn't help but be curious, so she asked her, "Help me out how?" Miz Lullabel answered real slow and careful-like. "It seem to me," she said, "like my mama had a sure-fire way of keeping a man doing your bidding for the rest of your days. I wouldn't tell this to just anybody, but you always been real special to me."

"What you got to do?" Miz Judson asked.

"Tonight when Brother Judson goes to bed, you go to

111

the drawer and get out your clipping shears. Go right up to his throat and cut off his whiskers. Put them whiskers in your shoe and walk all over that man! My mama would say that that is the onliest way of putting a man where you need 'em — underfoot, so he can do what you needs 'em to do!"

Miz Judson figured that it sounded like a pretty good plan, and it wasn't like it was gonna hurt nobody. "I'll do it," she said. "Sure enough, I'll do it." Miz Judson watched Miz Lullabel disappear on down the road, but what she didn't see was that Miz Lullabel had on a grin so wide, you could see every one of her five teeth! She didn't walk but a little ways 'fore she come up on Brother Judson out in the field arguing with his mule. When he saw Miz Lullabel Lee, he waved her on over. Miz Lullabel made her way to him and gave him a big howdy-do.

"Miz Lullabel Lee, I ain't seen you in . . . I don't know when. What are you doing way out here with the country folks?"

"Well now, Brother Judson, you know me to be a good Christian woman, and it seem like the Lord is steady trying to use me. Sometimes He gives me a message to carry on back to one of my folks, and last night He came to see me 'bout you. He told me something that's been a-worrying on me since it was delivered to me last night. I wouldn't've rightly believed it if He hadn't whispered it in my good ear to make sure I heard it just right."

"The Lord came by to see you 'bout me?" Brother Judson was as turned round as a hen with its head cut off. He couldn't rightly believe it. "Well, what did He say?"

"I don't mean to start no trouble," Miz Lullabel said, "but according to the Father hisself, your wife gonna try to

112

kill you tonight! She's gonna try to cut your throat! I declare," she said, "I couldn't rightly believe it, but He whispered it in my good ear. Since He told it to me, I ain't got no choice but to tell it to you."

"You must done gone crazy, Miz Lullabel Lee! They told me that you wear that wig too tight, and it seem like you done flipped it now! I been with that woman for more than fifty years. I ain't never seen better, and I done seen many. Now you standing there telling me that she's gonna kill me. She ain't got no reason to want to harm me. I work hard, love her easy, and don't even beat her! You must be 'bout crazy, that's what I say!"

Miz Lullabel wasn't the least put out by them carrying-on's. "You think what you want to," she said, "but if I were you, I'd sleep with one eye open tonight. I know plenty of folks resting six feet under 'cause they didn't listen to somebody they figured was crazy. Don't worry, I'm leaving now. I have done my duty. I might've brought the message, but it was the Almighty that was the messenger. You do what you want with the wisdoms, but if I were you I'd sleep with one eye open." With that Miz Lullabel Lee left and headed back to town. Now that grin was even wider. You could see every one of them teeth, and I do declare, she didn't have but four!

That night Mister Judson went to bed at the usual time. He told himself that he wasn't studying on nothing about what Miz Lullabel had said, but then he remembered what his daddy used to tell him: "You watch out for them colored women, son, you just never know what one of them's going do." So he pretended to sleep and started snoring real loud. Miz Judson, on hearing them loud snores, started grinning. Finally he was asleep, or so she thought. She climbed out of bed real careful-like so she wouldn't wake him. She didn't know Mister Judson was watching her every move. When she got to the drawer she found them clipping shears with no trouble at all. She turned around and walked over to her husband's throat so she could cut off some of them whiskers, put them in her shoe, and walk all over that man! But before she could start to cutting, Mister Judson jumped up and yelled loud enough for the whole world to hear, "They told me about you, and you sho' won't be killing me, not tonight!"

Sad to say, I hear they been fussin' ever since. Neighbors say that they sound like two alley cats fighting over a chicken bone.

Well, the next day Miz Lullabel Lee was a-setting on the porch, rocking back and forth. Once again, the Devil came riding on down the road on his horse. He stopped right in front of Miz Lullabel Lee's house, but he didn't get down off his horse, and he sure didn't get too close! He stood on back a ways. Miz Lullabel Lee wasn't bothered, not the least little bit. She was tickled.

"Devil," she said, "you ain't being too neighborly. Why don't you come and set awhile? I got a seat right here," and she pointed to her best chair. "I been expecting you," she said, and she grinned real wide so you could see every one of her teeth, and I do declare that's all she had — one!

"Oh no," said the Devil, shaking his head so hard you would've figured his horns would come off his head. "Any colored woman who can raise more hell than me is a dangerous woman, and I ain't got no business anywhere near 'em." With that he took the new hat and threw it clear through the air till it landed at her feet. And that Devil took off faster than the wind. Miz Lullabel didn't feel no shame, no shame at all. She picked up her new hat and pranced back and forth across the front porch.

The very next Sunday, Miz Lullabel picked out her prettiest dress and put it on. It went perfect with the new hat. She went to church and just showed out, I do tell you. There just ain't no understandin' that woman. She sat right behind the Judsons, and every time Sister Judson kicked Brother Judson or Brother Judson elbowed Sister Judson, Miz Lullabel Lee grinned a real big grin. Then she looked up at the heavens and asked, "Lord, now who said the Devil don't go to church?"

You see what I mean — evil is all around, everywhere you turn. That's why you can't let a whole lot of folks get to mixing in your stuff. Lord, the Devil sure is busy. Yessirree, always busy.

AFTERTHOUGHTS

Folk tales exist in every culture and for most of human history were the way of passing on wisdom from generation to generation. This oral tradition existed long before the written word, and it continues today. For many, the African American folk tale is synonymous exclusively with the Brer Rabbit tale. But we African Americans were far more creative than that, and we always gave the supernatural a free rein in our folklore. The Devil was frequently personified and made quite human; we taunted him as much as he taunted us, and often we emerged the victor.

The famous "John" stories are some of my favorite slave tales, as our ancestors created their own venues for besting their white masters, even if the victory was limited to their own imagination.

Folklorists such as Zora Neal Hurston and J. Mason Brewer were among the first African Americans to collect African American folklore and recognize its cultural significance. "Miz Lullabel, the Devil, and the Sunday Hat" was one of the tales collected by Zora Neal Hurston, but the story itself has been around a long time, and she herself didn't create it — she just documented the version she was told. Like any good storyteller, I have taken this tale and put my own twist on it.

When I perform this story, I always include an introduction that allows the listener to imagine those people and that place. "We're in North Carolina, and the year is nineteen twenty. We're sitting on the front porch, a bunch of country folks entertaining ourselves on a hot summer evening, when all of a sudden Miz Martha's sixteen-year-old daughter comes running down the walk as excited as excited can be. She's got big news, and she can't wait to share it.

"Mama, Mama, guess what, I'm getting married! I'm getting married, Mama — ain't that wonderful?"

Miz Martha then looks at her daughter and shakes her head in disbelief. "Girl, you don't know nothin' 'bout marriage. You can't take care of yourself, much less nobody else. You ain't got what it takes to be getting married."

But her daughter disagrees. "Yes I do, Mama. I got all I need. I got the man, the preacher, and the Kool-Aid — I'm getting married."

Miz Martha shakes her head again and then she says slowly, "Sit down, chile, I got some things to tell you. First, this thing called marriage is between you and him. If you let a third person in the middle of it, you've got nothin' but trouble. You got to understand that — and to make sure you do, I'm gonna tell you a story. Well, you see, one day Miz Lullabel was sittin' on the porch . . ." And so the truth-telling begins.

Lost Love, Last Love

Pauline and Jimmy. Jimmy and Pauline. Them two there was quite a pair, yessirree. Now Pauline was a sweet, sweet girl, and she sho' deserved better than Jimmy. I tells anybody who will listen that I ain't got no time for a man I got to raise 'fore I can love him. You just can't bring up no already grown man, 'cause that little bit you can give him as a woman ain't near 'nough to make up for what his mama ain't do for him when he was a boy. If you find a man that still got to be raised, well, you best to let him go on his way. That there ain't nothin' but a problem waitin' to happen.

Now, 'far as Jimmy went, I knew him 'fore he even knew hisself. He was my late husband's mother's second cousin's fourth son outta six — and even though he was kin, it didn't make me one bit of difference. He still wasn't no good — born on the wrong quarter of the moon, that's what I say. Soon as that boy started to smell hisself good, he was cuttin' up capers. I tell you, Old Man Satan must be the silent partner in the ownership of some folks, and he

118

had a strong hold on that one for sho'! He pranced around here like he was the only rooster who knew how to crow, and he didn't mind a-cock-a-doodle-dooing every chance he could get.

I tried to tell Pauline all this and then some, but she just wouldn't listen — nope, not to one single word. Jimmy was as long, lean, brown, and smooth as one of them fancy chocolate bars, and the minute Pauline laid eyes on him, I could see that she was busy tryin' to lick up every drop. She told me that she had to have him, and Lord bless her, she got him, too. Scarcely five months later, they was married right in her daddy's front yard. Well, maybe I should say that she was married but he sho' wasn't, 'cause 'fore the ink was even dry on them marriage papers, he'd already started slipping around. I don't know how he managed it with all that other that he had going on, but he got Pauline with four babies. One, two, three, four, and they come together, one right behind the other.

Since Jimmy was so busy spreadin' his lovin' from pillar to post, Pauline had to work two jobs just to keep that family going. Lord have mercy, she worked so very hard, but it still wasn't enough. What she couldn't do, the other women round here pitched in to help do. 'Course we had to sneak our helpin' out of the sight of Jimmy, 'cause he wouldn't do but didn't want nobody else to, neither. It sho' was a sad thing watchin' Pauline wear herself out like that for them children and that man. Seem like sometimes a woman's done got herself so low down till she ain't got sense enough to know she's been kicked or strength enough to get back up before she's licked. Yessirree, that was Pauline.

Now, as for Jimmy, he ain't never had no staying power.

He was like a feather tossed carelessly into the wind, a-driftin' here and there and never makin' it nowhere. So it wasn't no surprise to anyone here when we got word that Jimmy done made his way clear up to New York City. Told some folks that he had to go so he could make him some big money. Well, he must've gotten hisself lost with all them riches 'cause we ain't never seen any of it down here, nor did we see Jimmy hisself for ten years or more. He went on up there and found him a new somebody to rub up next to and a brand-new place to hang his britches. But God don't like ugly. "Sin," my mama used to say, "will sho' 'nough slow-walk you down."

Well, Jimmy got all that heartache throwed right back at him. After a while, he got sick, too sick to keep makin' the big money. And that hussy sent him right back to Pauline. She had chewed him up and spit him right back out when the sugar done gone. But Pauline was such a good girl and she turned out to be a fine woman, too, so when he showed up on her doorstep all broke-down and used-up, she took him right in. It must've been too late for Jimmy, though, 'cause he didn't last long. He was dead 'fore the month was out.

Of course, Pauline called me to help her with all the 'rangements. I was her friend and he was my kin, so I told her I would do whatever she wanted me to. I got to tell you, though, I done put away a whole lot of folks, but I ain't never seen nobody put away the way Jimmy was.

The morning that Jimmy passed, Pauline carried him on down to Joyner's Funeral Parlor. Actually, she didn't carry him the way most folks carry somebody. Rather, like, she dragged him! That man died right in her bed, and before the body could even get cold, Pauline had grabbed him by the shirt and commenced to draggin' the man directly down Main Street, the way you haul a full sack of cotton. Everybody's lookin' and she's steady draggin' Jimmy on behind her. She had this wild look in her eyes and the strength of two mules. Mr. Joyner told me that sometimes a crazy person will get every bit as strong as they is crazy, and I reckon that's what happened to Pauline.

I wish I could say that was the end of the madness, but sad to say, that was only the beginning. After she left Joyner's, I followed her back to the house, and there was a headstone a-settin' right in the middle of the floor.

"Pauline, have you lost your ever-lovin' mind?" I asked. "What's that doin' in here?"

"I don't believe in no last-minute shoppin'," she says. "I had Bill bring it on round when I saw Jimmy was fixin' to pass."

"But it ain't got no name on it, Pauline. You can't put no marker out that ain't got a name on it."

"You don't know as much as I thought you did," and then she looks at me like I'm the one outta my head. "If you put Jimmy's name on there, the Devil will find him for sure."

"Pauline, the Devil already done found Jimmy. They probably been hangin' out together all along. I'd be willing to bet you on that!" But no matter what I said, she still wouldn't listen, just walked on outta the room.

The next day things went even more cockeyed. I come out to the graveyard to find Pauline and to make sure everything was set for the service. There she was up in that tree that was overlookin' the grave, puttin' liquor bottles on every single limb!

"Pauline, what in blue blazes is you doing now? And where did you get all them liquor bottles? Girl, you don't even drink!"

"The kids got 'em for me. It took 'em a good while, though, 'cause they got to go through every trash can in town to get all I needed, but here they is. Ain't they something?" Then she smiled and went on back to decorating.

"Pauline, I ain't never seen nothin' like this in all my life."

"When the soul rises up it goes to what it know, and all that joker ever knew was a liquor bottle and a good time. When he gets ready to leave this time, he won't get too far. Ain't no way he'll pass all this Jack Black, and then I got him! I sho' do. I got him."

I didn't want to upset her 'cause in the state of mind she was in, there was no tellin' what she might do so I left the liquor bottles and Miz Pauline alone. The service went fine, though, and that was a blessing. Not too many there, but the few that were there were a nice surprise. Afterward, I thought it would be best if Pauline went back to the house and rested herself a bit, and I said so. But what did she do? She and them four young'uns climbed up in that tree and commenced to picking them liquor bottles off the limbs.

"Pauline," I said, real quiet-like, "what are you going to do with all them bottles?"

"Take 'em home, of course."

"What for, sweetie? The service is over now."

"For the first time in more than ten years, I have my husband back, and he ain't gettin' away easy this time. I figure I'll put this Jack Black right next to my bed 'cause I just know a little piece of him is in there. Now when I leave this world, you can let him leave, too. Hopefully, though, we'll be going in two different directions, if you know what I mean." Then she winked at me and strutted happily down the road.

Later that month I went on by to check on her. I rang the back doorbell and waited. 'Course them liquor bottles were still there a-staring at me, but I didn't pay them no mind. Pauline come out lookin' like a million dollars, and I was sho' glad that she was doing so much better.

"Girl, you sho' is lookin' good," I told her.

"Ain't nothin' like havin' a man around again. Chile, there ain't nothin' like that."

"You got a man? You don't say. Who is he? Do I know him?"

"You so crazy," she said with a laugh. "It's Jimmy, of course. Did you say hi to him? You'll hurt his feelings if you don't at least speak." And then she looked down at all them liquor bottles. Well, just then Mister Jones comes up to drop off the milk she had asked for. Pauline grabbed the milk and was headin' in the house. "Y'all go 'head and visit with Jimmy. I'll be right back," and in a lickety-split she was gone. I looked over at Mister Jones and he looked at me. Then he looked down at all them liquor bottles scattered hither and yonder. Now, Mister Jones got plenty of good sense. "Jimmy?" he asked. "There ain't no Jimmy here. What in the world is she talkin' about?"

"Please don't ask no questions," I begged him. "Whatever you do, just don't ask one thing. Just say, 'Hey, Jimmy,' and keep on going, but please don't ask no questions."

Well, he did just that and then he left with the oddest look on his face that I ever did see. Love sho' can do strange things to folks, can't it?

Yessirree, strange, strange things.

AFTERTHOUGHTS

Bottle trees like the one mentioned in my story are a reality that is clearly the product of Southern black culture. Once a frequent sight along the Mason-Dixon landscape, bottle trees today are a rarity and are as likely to be produced by rural whites as by blacks. Now they are simply remnants of an innovative past, yet another example of the ingenuity of black folks as they re-created themselves many years ago on this land, then foreign to them.

Bottle trees were a part of a rich African legacy, a folk-art tradition with roots a thousand years deep. As early as the year 900 A.D., Africans made bottles and other forms of glass art and hung these objects on trees and huts to ward off evil. African Americans retained the tradition and often hung their bottles on cedar-tree branches to trap unwelcome spirits. When the wind blew, so the story goes, the spirits moaned and cried long into the night. Sunlight dancing through colored glass has been a fascination for people for generations, and these prisms were obviously bright spots in a sometimes otherwise bleak existence. Given the spiritual significance of this wonderful folk art, perhaps Pauline was on to something after all. Maybe, just maybe, a li'l piece of Jimmy's soul was indeed captured by that Jack Black bottle. We may never know for sure.

The Bluesman

It was raining, the sound drumming softly through the room, dripping and shattering like large teardrops. The big black man looked out the window and stared aimlessly into the dreary evening. He took another gulp of bathtub gin, trying once again to drown out the bleakness that seemed to surround him. Despite his best efforts (three full glasses of Mister Jim's real good stuff), he realized that he was still sinking further and further into the dark hole he called his soul. He knew it wouldn't be long now before he reached rock bottom.

He could go on across the hall and seek some small comfort in the loving arms of the beautiful woman he called Lady. No names, he'd insisted when they'd first met. Even when she'd tried to press him for some small clue to his identity, he would give nothing away, so she remained Lady and he would forever more be her Song Man. She'd wandered into his life two nights ago (or was it three?) in a cloud of smoke, laughter, and cheap perfume; he had been alone and so was she, so why not be alone together? Why not indeed? His hand shook and the ice clinked together softly. Alone together — some would say that that was an impossibility, but the big black man who lingered sadly in the shadows knew that not only was it possible, it was the story of his existence. He'd spent what seemed to be an entire life trying to bury loneliness and despair in a sea of waiting audiences, momentary pleasures, and lowly song lyrics.

Alone with someone together. That might be kind of nice about now. He wondered what his Lady would do if he sauntered on across the hall and suggested that they try it for the evening. He laughed and then stumbled. Maybe that wouldn't be such a good idea after all. He was a lot more tore up than he thought. Nobody needed to be anywhere near him when he was like this. Best if he stayed alone alone this evening.

He did have another woman. She wasn't new or novel, however, like the one 'cross the hall. Hell, he'd known Estella Mae since the cow jumped over the moon. 'Course, long time knowing didn't guarantee any real understanding 'cause he could no more figure that woman than he could predict the makeup of the Lord's next day.

Folks liked to call her his regular. He supposed "regular" was accurate enough, considering that when after all was said and done, he always somehow managed to end up right back to her. Now 'course, comin' around every now and again for some occasional good loving was 'bout "regular" as it ever got, and 'bout regular as it was ever likely to be. He knew from the hopeful looks she threw his way that she would have preferred a more formal understanding, but he also knew deep down in his heart that would never be. He was fond of her, sure — after ten years of comfortable companionship he could freely admit to that much. From time to time he even missed her when she wasn't near, but love had been his reality only once, and it had been for a woman who now lived in another place and another time. There was simply no looking back. He wasn't sure he would even if he could.

He looked longingly 'cross the hall. His daddy used to say that every town suplied its own women and its own opportunities; and now after years of drifting *he* knew that better than most. His woman back home wouldn't like it — him messing around and all, but that was really too bad. She would have to just content herself with being "regular" and leave that other business for his tending to.

He wondered if the woman 'cross the hall was one of those kind that would be looking for him to be somebody he wasn't, and saying a whole lot of stuff he surely wouldn't mean. If they did get together tonight, that was all that it would be, because tomorrow he would surely be gone to yet another place with its own beautiful women. He smiled as he thought of what Miss "Regular" would do if she found out about Miss "Tonight." He'd seen that temper of hers — not too often, mind you, but enough to know that whenever it came around, it was best to get out of its way. The screaming and yelling weren't too bad, but the minute her hands took hold of her hips, and her head started bobbing and weaving like something possessed, well, he made tracks to the nearest door. She'd told him once that if he cheated on her, he'd best to make hisself scarce 'cause she was going to take him clear on outta this world. He laughed and told her that wasn't no woman ever gonna get the best of him so she'd best forget them crazy rantings and ravings. She didn't like that though — commenced to rolling her eyes so 'til he thought they'd roll clear out of her head. Women! Lord, they were troublesome.

He walked over to the bed intending to lay down easy, but instead found himself falling down hard, so hard that the punch almost sobered him — but, alas, no such luck, because soon he was once again floating happily in a gin-filled fog. The rain seemed to be stopping. He'd figured correctly that since it had started out as hard as it did, it probably wouldn't last too long. He looked out the window again and noticed that the dreariness was already drying up. Now the night looked like one big lazy picture that seemed far, far away. It was as if he was one place and the rest of the world was another. How many times over the last couple of years had he done this? he wondered — laying around in dingy little rooms that would be home for the minute; disappearing from reality one gulp at a time and endlessly drifting between hunger pains and frustrated sighs.

On the road they called him the Night Hawk. Like a loose and restless blackbird he haunted the nights with his sad, sad tunes. His music was his life, or maybe he played out his life in his music. Or maybe his music and his life had long ago merged into one long melancholy melody.

He played for anybody who cared to listen. He didn't need anything more than a place to sit, the guitar he called Indigo, and an invitation. Sometimes he didn't wait for the invitation. Once, he tried desperately to silence the madness, vowing never ever to play again, but that didn't last long. Somehow or another the demon had gotten free again. After that he kept his music closer to him, nestled nearer to his gut, unleashing pieces of it slow and easy. Folks listening to him always said that when he played, it was like somebody dishing out something strong and sweet one spoonful at a time. He would eventually satisfy your hunger, but he never quite emptied his pot. He always held something back. Maybe it was that special portion that was supposed to be only his.

He wondered what it would be like to die. Would it be like this — a remote, dreary silence that seemed to go on and on — or would he finally be sucked into that abysmal black hole once and for all? He finished his glass of gin, tasting some and spilling most, and then sat the empty glass on the floor next to him. He was about to drift off to sleep when he heard a nightingale outside his window singing his little heart out. Poor little fellow, he thought. I know just how he feels.

One Uppity Blues Woman

The drink house was small, dark, smoky, and noisy. Still, people managed to chat happily with one another, and laughter rippled loudly throughout, assuring Mister Jim that people were indeed having a good time. A sea of moonshine was flowing about freely, and Mister Jim could see that his patrons were gloriously wading deep, deep into their cups. It was the same each and every night since he'd opened up his home twelve years ago to the wandering coloreds who roamed the nighttime hours looking for some company and maybe a little relief from the day-to-day hardships. There were now several other drink houses in town, but his was the hands-down favorite because at his place the drinks were strong, the good times were cheap, and the music was steaming hot.

In the back of the drink house sat a colored woman boldly admiring a handsome man at a table on the far side of the room. He was a pretty-colored brown (not too black, she didn't even look at a man darker than brandy), and he was tall, she could tell that even though he was sitting down. He had on a tan straw hat cocked arrogantly to one side, so dangerously tilted that on a lesser man it would have surely fallen to the floor, but on this man it didn't dare.

He had a drink in his hand that he sipped slowly and carefully, kinda lazy and easy-like. A man who sipped that leisurely and tenderly would probably love a woman the same way, she thought. She was tempted to get up, cross on over, and plant herself right next to him, but she quickly realized that her liquor was already doing its job. It had completed the slow burn to her gut and was now pounding in her head but was at least dispensing its usual goodwill — that numbing kind of listlessness that prevents one from thinking too deeply, caring too much, or moving too quickly.

She continued to stare, and eventually the force of her observation turned his head in her direction. They locked eyes for a minute and then smiled at one another. She issued a grin of invitation, one he obviously decided not to accept. Still, he nodded his head in polite appreciation, and damn it if that hat didn't stay put. It was probably for the best, though, his saying no and all. She was still wearing the troubles from the last man, the burden of grief weighing heavily upon her like lead. Her lover was dead; a blues-singing man silenced forever more. This evening she would mourn her man in the only way she knew how.

* * *

131

Well, there was no doubt about it, the woman dazzling the crowd was as talented as everybody had said, and uglier than anybody could have imagined.

People have different blues
and I think they're mighty sad,
But the blues about a man
the worst I've ever had,
I get all disgusted and all confused
Every time I look around, yonder comes the blues.

Even the amber-glowing lanterns filling the place with soft, golden beauty did nothing to gentle her homeliness. She was short, and, mercy, she was fat too — real fat. Now, if Sister Minnie had been there, she would have insisted that a mite more polite description be used, like "smallish in stature and pleasingly plump." Now, that may have sounded nicer to the ear, but it would in no way match up to the woman sashaying before her eyes. True, she was no more than five feet tall, but everything about her screamed big, too big really for just one woman. Her mama always said that everybody had their own beauty and it would eventually show itself if you waited long enough, but if there was something beautiful about this woman, it still hadn't made an appearance and the show was 'bout over.

Now, if Little Boy Willy had been there, he would have looked at the unappealing face with the too-large features (a nose so wide it should have been made to carry a permit to travel clear 'cross her face the way it did, a big-lipped grin of oversized crooked gold teeth, luminous brown eyes that would make a spook owl envious, and all of it capped off with a wild, wiry mane that managed somehow or another to stand out in every direction at once). Well, Little Boy Willy would have just called a spade a spade and proclaimed with sound authority that the woman was just plain butt-ugly. Lucy Mae would have looked at all that greasepaint covering her face in an attempt to make the complexion underneath appear lighter, and she would have said loud enough for the dead to take notice, that "it don't much matter how much you whitewash the pot, that black is still there." Now, Miss Bessie would have probably been more discreet with her observations, preferring instead to cast shy, disdainful glances in the direction of the now wiggling, jiggling mass strutting across the stage, and Miss Bessie would have whispered for select ears only that "the woman was so fat her man probably had to grab hold of her on the installment plan." 'Course, it would have been Jimmy who would have, as always, had to have the last word. "I declare that woman is so black, she could get a job with the government spitting ink." But none of them folks were nowhere 'round.

> *I'm a big fat mama*
> *and I got the meat shaking on my bones*
> *And every time I shake*
> *Some skinny gal gonna lose her home . . .*

The crowd roared with laughter, and obviously the men had managed to forge past the hopelessly unattractive exterior and must have found for themselves that elusive beauty her mama was talking about, because they now whistled appreciatively and watched her gracefully moving behind with flirtatious bedroom eyes. Ma Rainey was singing her heart out, and the colored woman watched in fascination. Ma Rainey always said that she sang her blues for the sisters because "the blues wasn't nothing more than a good woman feeling bad," and for the sad colored woman who mourned the loss of a soulful lover, Ma Rainey was telling the absolute truth.

AFTERTHOUGHTS

In the 1890s, several new musical forms arose in the black communities of the South. One of these new forms was the blues. Blues came directly from the rural communities, and the basic vocal material for early folk blues came from field hollers and work songs. Sharecroppers, hoping to escape the drudgery of life on worn-out tiny plots of farmland, watched with growing frustrations as their hopes were dashed time and time again, and put their dissatisfaction to music.

During the 1890s, most show songs were humorous, sentimental, or tragic, often depicting strong nostalgia or romantic love, but blues was different. Although blues spoke freely on the complex relationships between men and women, it did not avoid subjects like sickness, death, misery, crime, and social/political/economic injustices. It avoided religion like the plague but felt free to tangle with a preacher, the devil, or one of the church's supposedly saintly women. Prayers were statements of faith, hopes that one day things would be all right, but the blues was the way of telling the Lord exactly what was wrong.

For me, the blues strikes a personal chord. It moves me in ways I can't begin to articulate. It takes my sorrows and makes them tangible so I can wrestle with them for a while before I can turn 'em loose to the heavens. Blues lets me laugh about ordinary troubles and remember the more profound problems that haunt some others. There's nothing like the blues, and I remember, oh so well, the first time I heard it up close and personal.

It was sort of like a tent show. The man who was going to sing stood up and commanded everybody's attention. There was a lantern next to him and it cast a warm glow across his face. He hadn't done anything yet, but everyone could see that he was drenched in perspiration. His eyes were closed as if he was trying to remain oblivious to everyone there. After a few seconds he took a deep breath and then another. He was clearly working his way up to something, but he seemed to be in no hurry to get there. The audience waited patiently. We knew there was no point in trying to rush him. Our time was his and we silently gave him our permission to do it with it as he saw fit.

He reached over into the darkness and lifted up his guitar. It wasn't the fanciest, but it would do. His eyes were opened slightly and his tongue was working its way slowly across his lips to moisten them sufficiently for the work they would need to do. Somebody brought the man a stool and he sat down quietly. The stool was obviously not built to hold a man his size and he looked as if he would topple at any moment, but he squirmed around until he found the perfect balance. He placed the guitar in front of him and it looked ridiculously inadequate, this small guitar in front of such a big man, but it would hold its own.

His hands moved over the instrument and he began to play. As large as his fingers were, you wouldn't expect them to be so nimble, so quick, or so sensual, but they were all that and more. They stroked and they teased. They demanded and they gave and the results, well, the results were heart-wrenching sobs that sang to every soul there. Long piercing sounds created to tug on a person's core, holding on to you so tight 'til you felt like they would never let go. And just when you thought you couldn't be pulled any tighter, they snapped and let you sail away free. When the blues man started to sing, the words started out as barely a whisper. Some of them you couldn't quite make out, but it didn't matter. The lyrics were poignant and questioning, sometimes sad, but other times surprisingly funny. Now several people in the room closed their eyes and swayed to the music. We were all of one accord, moving together, feeling together, and testifying together. The next song was slower and had no words at all, just moans, hums, and music. It knocked you down, dragged you around, and then in the end, it lifted you back up again. We all felt like we'd been through the wringer, all used up but nowhere near through.

That was my first experience with the blues and I've been hooked ever since. Maybe as a storyteller I'm drawn to the moving narratives and wonderful tales I find make up the core of their songs. I just wish that I could sing because I declare, there are moments I would just go ahead and join right on in.

Young Folks

The Colored Water Fountain

Martha rose early this Saturday morning. It was her sixth birthday and it was a very special day, not only because on this sunny day in 1955 she was now six, but also because she would get to go with Papa into town. Town was really a big bustling place — the city of Birmingham, Alabama.

There were lots of pretty little shops, restaurants, and people, people everywhere. Her brothers and sisters had already filled her in on all the exciting things to do and see, and she could hardly wait.

She brushed her teeth an extra dozen times just to be sure they were at their sparkling best, picked out her prettiest dress, twirled around in it at least six times, and ate an extra bowl of oatmeal for energy. Papa was ready to go as soon as she wolfed down the last little drop. She raced out the door and sat next to him on the front seat. What a day this was going to be!

Papa sat tall and straight and whistled some of his

favorite church hymns to pass the time on the long drive. He whistled, she hummed, and sometimes they sang together. On the last song, though, they had both somehow forgotten the words, so they looked at each other shame-faced and then giggled until their sides hurt. Papa always looked so handsome when he laughed — 'course with these tough times, sure wasn't much to smile about, but Papa always managed to somehow be of good cheer.

When Papa parked carefully in front of the General Store, Martha raced out of the car before it had even come to a complete stop. This was the place! She ran over to the water fountains. One said W-H-I-T-E-S. That was not the one. The other said, C-O-L-O-R-E-D. That was it — the one she was looking for. She pushed the button hard and fast. She couldn't wait to see the colored water. She wondered if it would sparkle as brilliantly as a rainbow after a good summer rain. She pushed and she pushed, but nothing came forth but ordinary drinking water. She looked up at her father, who had followed her quietly to the fountain. She could see in his face that he was confused, but what she couldn't understand was why. Surely Papa knew all about the pretty colored water — why, there were signs that said C-O-L-O-R-E-D all over town.

"Papa, where is the pretty water?" she asked softly.

"What pretty water, Martha?"

"The colored water that sparkles like rainbows — see, right there, it says C-O-L-O-R-E-D." She was so proud that she could read such a big word that she pointed right to it, so's to really show off. She was smiling — at least at first, or at least until she saw her daddy look down to the ground, shuffling his feet back and forth and paining to say something that must be gonna hurt pretty bad.

"Something wrong, Daddy?" she asked.

He was real quiet, and she thought she saw tears in his eyes, but Lord, that couldn't be — Daddy never cried, 'specially not over something simple like some colored water.

"Martha, my sweet, baby girl," he began slowly. "That sign ain't got nothin' to do with somethin' as beautiful as one of God's rainbows. That there got to do with somethin' mean and ugly — some sin-filled evil ones that think that the color of your skin got to do with who you are and what you mean to the Father above. That there," he said, getting really angry now, "says that you, me, and all of our kind ain't good as white, not now or ever. It means that no matter what you do in this world, it won't never be good enough, 'cause all Birmingham is ever gonna see is another nigger in America. That's all there is to that there." And he walked stiffly into the store.

Martha stood there looking at her daddy's back for a moment and then back to the fountain. Somehow she just wasn't thirsty anymore. Later, when they arrived home, Martha looked at her birthday presents. Mama had got her the books she'd wanted — all those wonderful fairy tales, "Snow White," "Sleeping Beauty," and "Goldilocks." She had wanted them so badly, but now — well, things were looking very different than they had yesterday. Slowly, carefully, and quite deliberately, she tore each one to shreds. What was the point? There was no Prince Charming riding into her future, nor would there be anyone to rescue her from her troubles, not now or ever. Her kinky hair, too-black face, and thick lips would never be anybody's idea of beauty, neither. She was just another nigger in America, and the time to stop dreaming was now. The tears welled in her eyes, but she refused to let them fall — that would just have to wait till another day, another day that was probably a long way away.

AFTERTHOUGHTS

Jim Crow, the familiar term for the subordination and separation of African Americans in the South, began during Reconstruction and continued until the conclusion of the freedom movement. Some of Jim Crow was legislated but much of it was enforced by custom and practice. Everybody knew their place, and in the early part of the twentieth century few ventured outside of those approved spaces.

White Southerners lived by a strict racial creed. It was based on two main principles; black inferiority and white supremacy. It was a painful combination of paternalism and Negrophobia (an intense fear of black men) and denied African Americans even the remotest opportunities for happiness. It stripped them of all dignity and respect, and I remember, oh so well, the stories that my father used to tell about growing up in Alabama during the 1930s and '40s. Walk along the road, he said, and you see a white man coming toward you, then you'd better lower your eyes and cross over to the other side. Venture out on a Saturday to treat yourself to a dandy new hat and you'd better pick carefully because anything you tried on you owned, 'cause no white person would wear anything after it had been touched by somebody black.

It was so dehumanizing, my dad would recall with that faraway look in his eyes, and that horrible senseless system of hatred didn't even have the decency to spare the children. It pressed itself down on the backs of our innocence like a tarnished lead anchor. My dad would say: "There just ain't nothing worse than having somebody look at you like something they wanted scraped off the bottom of their shoe and then trying for the life of you to figure out what in the world you ever did that could make somebody hate you so much." He always ended with a long weary sigh. "I don't suppose some of us will ever get over it."

NOBODY'S CHILE

You know when I was little,
we slept three to a bed, four to the floor,
two at the door, and we prayed like the dickens
Mama and Daddy wouldn't have no more.
Back then, babies were made on dream-filled beds
found in tilting old shacks,
built of not much more than ticks and tacks
but we managed to keep it all together with faith and love,
and an occasional miracle from up above.

You know when I was little
school was learning to read with a hoe and write with a plow,
and I remember oh so well
that the lovin' could be hard, the livin' could be hell,
the Devil could walk like a man
and Papa's liquor could sound mighty darn loud
when you gave it a tug and it got loose from the jug,
but the understandin' was

that you stayed out of white folks' business,
grown folks' conversations, and niggers' no good mess.

Chile, when I was little,
pig lard greased your hair, a croaker sack warmed your back
and Mother Earth was the shoes that wore your feet black.
Miss Sally Walker could rise, the game was Miss Mary Mack,
the animals talked, wisdom walked,
and Bur Rabbit was the know-it-all in this here town.
Each and every spring, the May pole would go round and round
and a chile's joy was a blessing — wherever it could be found.

You know when I was little
pennies never quite made it from Heaven
but were grudgingly pinched from some white man's pants pocket.
Santa rarely made it.
So Christmas was usually just an apple dangling down from a tree
and New Year's was yet another maybe.

Baby, when I was little,
Mister Charlie decided that I wasn't too small,
that my body was already well into its prime,
my virtue was up for grabs,
and that his needs were far more important than mine.
So at thirteen, I became a white man's whore
and suddenly I wasn't so little no more.

You know when I was little
I found out that nobody could afford to give me a childhood,
that not knowing could be way too dangerous
and innocence was reserved for little white girls
with big blue eyes and long blond curls.

I realized early on that Ishmael's tears may have moved God to
goodness and mercy,
but mine just made me old and ugly,
and mercy was a promise for yet another day
that reigned up in Heaven, a million miles away.

Chile, when I was little,
it sure was tough to be somebody's colored baby
in this here old place.
And gracious, from where I'm a-settin',
it don't look like things done changed up they face.

Hush-a-Bye

In a little girl's lonely world, the corn stalks rustled like a snake's wicked rattler, the moon danced ominously through the dark oak trees, and the winds whispered warnings to anyone who would dare to be out on such a night. But caution fell upon stubborn ears. Ruth could not allow herself to be dissuaded. She might have only been ten, but she was soon to be a saint, and she had been sent seeking the truth. If Jesus was here, she would find Him. She would not leave this place until she did.

The mothers had lovingly prepared her, as they did all who were about to take this journey. The moment the blood had flowed through her legs, taking her into the wonderful world of womanhood, the mothers had begun their ritual. She had been taken down to the river's edge, scrubbed clean of past sin, and readied to be born again in the spirit. Mother Faye was chosen to be her guide. Together they had prayed, but separately they would see the light. When the brilliant deliverance had come and gone,

Ruth would be allowed to return and take her rightful place on the holy pew. She would wear a little white hat that the women would embroider. She would rest among the blessed and speak in the tongues of the saved. She would never be the same again, they had told her, and for the little girl who was really nobody's chile but everybody's baby, this promise was a miracle that was only days away.

Although she was nobody's chile, she did have someone who loved her. Nana cared for her like she was truly her own. Ruth would ask her over and over again how she came to be hers, and Nana loved to tell the story, loved to remember that day, over ten years ago, when she'd found a precious li'l baby layin' in the middle of the meadow — bloomin' and blossomin' without love, tenderness, or care. A beautiful li'l baby who refused to surrender to the harshness of her reality but instead decided to shine like a morning glory. A precious little one who refused to be frightened and did not utter a single sound. A baby who had been waitin' for a mama, and a woman who was waitin' to *be* a mama. They needed each other then, and they needed each other now. Nana was counting on Ruth to save her, and Ruth refused to let Nana down.

Nana, on her sickbed, was ready to leave this world and enter the next. This morning they had come, as Nana's eyes rolled around her head, and her mouth made funny little sounds, and they had prepared for her death. The mirrors had been covered and the pillows removed from the back of her head. Brother Jake had stood continuously in the middle of the room singin' hymns, and the saints, well, they had rocked and prayed. They would sit up with Nana until it was all over, and then Pastor Brown would anoint her with the special oil he kept in his pocket. The evangelists would come soon after and dress her.

They would put on her very best suit and the ugly black shoes that her Sister Hessie had given her. Nana had told Sister Hessie, on one of her last goods days, that she didn't want to be put away in those shoes, but Sister Hessie wouldn't listen. She would put on the dark suit that she liked rather than the red dress Nana preferred. And then she would put on those ugly old-lady black shoes, and grin a real big toothless grin, just 'cause they were new. They had belonged to another, but that saint had died 'fore she had a chance to wear 'em, lucky her! "Why waste good shoes?" Sister Hessie had asked, "especially since they ain't but one size too big for Nana's size-six feet." But Nana had warned that when you wear somebody else's shoes to be buried in, they pinch your toes all the way to Heaven, and Nana wanted a comfortable trip. Sister Hessie would never listen, though — she would bury Nana as she saw fit, and poor old Nana would probably stumble her way on through the Lord's pearly gates. Well, Ruth might have been only ten, but she was sure big enough to save Nana. She would simply ask Jesus to spare Nana, so that she would have someone she could love. She would meet Jesus here, and she would beg him. She was not too proud to do that.

Not more than a year ago, she and Nana had huddled together at the little wood stove. Ruth remembered it like it was yesterday. Nana stood steady, strugglin' to infuse a li'l discipline into Ruth's wayward head of hair — tuggin' the hissin' hot comb through each carefully parted section, and Ruth flinchin' as the comb made its way, inch by inch, through the resistant locks. This had been their routine each and every Saturday evenin' after the supper dishes were done. But one evenin' had been real special.

"Nana, do you think Jesus can really love somebody like me?"

"Chile, what kind of question is that? Just last week in Sunday school, they taught you my favorite song, 'Jesus Loves Me, This I Know.' That song there ought to tell you what you needs to know. You think we'd be singin' that in church and all if it wasn't true? My mama used to say that God done made all of us, and He don't make no junk."

"Well," Ruth said, "Jessie says that Jesus ain't got no use for no ugly li'l black girl like me. She say that's why my mama, whoever she be, left me in the middle of a field like a pile of trash she want throwed away, 'cause she looked at me and decided she ain't had no use for nothing' that looked like me. Just 'cause I beat Jessie Lee at the spelling bee last Thursday, and ain't nobody ever done that before, she got to go and say all that. And that not all Jessie Lee say, she say —"

Nana just shook her head and said, "Jessie Lee say this, and Jessie Lee say that. Her lips ain't no prayer book, and her tongue is loose on both ends. Fact is, the Lord brung us together 'cause He knew I could love you better than anybody. Sometimes a mama is buried so deep in her own hurtin' that she can't do right by no chile. She got to heal herself 'fore she can tend to another, and the Lord makes sure she gets that time. Yo' mama left you out there 'cause she knew somebody would find you — and that somebody was me. I thank God every day for you. You know what the preachers always say, don't you? 'What God done brung together, let no man tear apart' — and that mean Jessie Lee, too."

"Nana, they say that for marryin'," Ruth giggled.

"It ain't just for no marryin', neither, it's for any joinin' up. God done brought us together, and ain't nobody got nothin' to say 'bout it. Now bend your head so I can get through."

Nana loved her. Ruth might be nobody's chile, but she was Nana's own. Nana had told her that she was as black and pretty as a thousand summer-midnight skies. Nana looked at her with all the love of any mama. Nana, bless her heart, had never given Ruth nothing but love and kindness. But now she might be leavin' this world, and Ruth would once again be alone.

"Look for the light," Nana had told her. "When it comes to seekin', look for the light. It will let you know that the Lord has looked into your heart and saved your soul. Just look for that light. It could come as a flicker, a sparkle, or even a blast. But you'll know it when you see it, and what a glorious day that will be. I can tell you that I seen that light at twelve, and it ain't never growed dim. Dark roads and bleak nights don't even worry me no more 'cause I still got the light. The light, Ruthy Ann, look for the light!"

Well, if Nana was right, then the Lord would be here tonight and would wrap his arms on around Ruth Ann Williams. He would touch her in a mighty way, and He would answer her prayers to restore Nana to good health and strength. She would know, then, that she would never again have nothin' to fear as long as she held on to the light. Ruth, like all the others who had come before to the wilderness, the chosen ones who had set in the plain and simple, who knew how to get still and quiet so they could hear the voice of God, would find all that she was lookin' for.

The winds were beginning to gust quite a bit now. Ruth pulled her wrapper a li'l tighter around her. She had been squattin' so long her legs had gone to sleep. She rocked on her heels a little to see if she could restore some feeling to her numb little limbs. An ant was makin' its way slowly up her thigh and would probably bite her if she didn't kill him. She let him be — tonight was not the night for killing. She closed her eyes. She would open them again only after she had been visited by the greatness. It would come, too, just like Nana had said it would — to a li'l black girl sittin' in the openness. She had found love once before in the middle of the field, and she would do so again. She rocked harder and faster and then she began to sing. He was on the way, Ruth reminded herself. Salvation was now only a breath away. Serenity was beginning to surround her. He would be here soon, and Ruth would be ready. Yes, she would be ready for Him when He came.

Little Boy Blue

Junior looked out his door real quiet-like. He had eased it open just enough so he could hear a little but not enough so he could be seen. The wooden floor in the little cabin was always so cold this time of year; it made his feet ache to walk on it. His grandma had bought him some new slippers with the money she'd made from takin' in two extra loads of wash last week, but he didn't bother to put them on. He might be heard, and he didn't want that. His mama would light into him but good if she thought he was standing in the middle of somethin' he ain't had no business in.

Shadows danced through the poorly lit room, and his mama was way 'cross to the other side, but Junior could see her good enough, and she didn't have on nothin' but a slip. She was sippin' whiskey out of a coffee cup. Junior might have only been six, but he'd seen a lot in his years, and he knew whiskey when he saw it in Mama's half-closed eyes or heard it slur 'cross her lips. The man that was standin' next to her had on pants but no shirt. He had a tattoo on his arm that looked like a snake, and his white hand grabbin' hold of Mama's arm made Mama look black as coal. That man had been there before. He always came in late and left 'fore morning. Junior always knew when he was around 'cause he smoked them smelly "roll-your-owns," and the stench of 'em always woke Junior clear out of a good sleep. The man's hand lifted up to his mama's breast and he squeezed it real hard.

"Ain't you had enough?" His mama asked the man, and then she laughed a fake laugh. Junior always knew she was fakin' happiness 'cause the smile never quite made it up to her eyes. The eyes, Junior figured, never hid a thing.

"I ain't never got enough, but it'll have to do 'cause I got to go. Sue will be lookin' for me soon, and I don't want her lookin' too hard."

"You know," Junior's mama began slowly, "I figured you might be able to spare a few dollars. Junior's birthday is tomorrow, and he got his eye on this little checker set — I thought maybe . . . ," and her voice faded away.

"Didn't I just give you some money?"

"That was over a month ago. That money been gone. I was just thinkin' . . ."

"You ain't supposed to be thinkin' nothin'. I ain't got no money for no checker set. My boy need him a new fishin' pole, and I barely got enough for that."

"But you got two boys," his mama pleaded. Junior hated to see his mama beggin'. "One might live on Hill Top, and the other on the Bottoms, but they both your boys. Junior got his heart as hard on that checker set as that other one got his on that fishin' pole. Since you missed Junior's

Christmas on account of your boy needin' that new bike, I thought maybe since it's his birthday and all —"

"Don't be countin' the money in my pocket. It ain't yours to be figurin'. Don't none of what go on at Hill Top need to reach down here to you. You just make sure you here when I say be here, and keep your mouth shut. The rest will take care of itself. As for that boy of yours, he gonna have to wait. What's a nigger boy need with a checker set anyway? Maybe you ought to bring him on out to my tobacco field so he can help put in my crop. I need some help, and that boy of mine seem to be too busy with that new bike of his to do me much good. Yeah, you bring that kid of yours on over and I'll get him started. Oh, and here's a quarter. See what you can do with that."

Junior closed the door softly and then went back to bed. He lay down and pretended to sleep till mornin' came and his mama shook him to get up.

"Happy birthday, baby. Mama got a big surprise for you — a brand-new quarter to spend at the General Store. I know you'll like that — and after we leave there I got somebody special for you to meet. He's kind of a friend of mine. He gonna show you all about farmin'." And then she hugged him. Junior took the quarter 'cause he didn't want to hurt his mama's feelin's. He smiled up at her, too — only he wondered if that smile ever made it up to his eyes.

Little Cinder Lea

Lea opened her eyes slowly. It was still dark out, but the sun would be rising at any time now, and so should she. It was Wednesday; no, maybe Thursday — Lea just couldn't remember. Every day seemed to be just like any other. Lea wasn't but twelve, but today she felt like she was a hundred and twelve. She'd told Miz Mayfield that her room was drafty on account of the wind that was breezin' right on in the cracked window, but Miz Mayfield didn't care. Just told her to stuff a rag in the crack and let it be. But when it was really windy, or rainy — and it had been both last night — the rag somehow made its way loose and the damp cold crept through Lea's bones slowly and surely. She had taken two doses of castor oil just yesterday to try to rid her body of the cold that left her achin' and painin', but it hadn't helped much. Mama said it would, but it didn't.

Mama. Lea sure wished she could see her mama today, even if it was only for a moment. She wished she could reach out and touch her, or better yet, hug her around the neck real tight like she used to when she was just a little girl. Sometimes the memory of being a child seemed like a fantasy that lived a thousand years ago, but it had been only five or six years since she had been able to awaken each day, roll over, and snuggle closed to her mama, and then get up and fix the family grits, with Mama's keen eye watchin' all the while to make sure she didn't make 'em to stiff or too soupy. Everybody would gather round the table, say grace, and eat together before the younger ones headed to school each day. No matter what, Mama would say, "school was a must." But now it had been three years since Lea had seen the inside of a schoolroom. Her days were spent miserably tendin' to Miz Mayfield and her lazy brood.

Would it be easier, she wondered, if she jumped up quick and faced the cold darkness all at once, or eased into the discomfort a little at a time? She stuck her toes out from under the covers and then quickly pulled them back in. Lord, but it was cold. She did have a little fireplace in her room, but cut wood was in such short supply that Miz Mayfield had said she would just have to do without until there was some extra. The nightshirt she had been given to wear was so raggedy that it invited the cool air in to dance mockingly through the useless garment. Even after she washed at the washbowl and dressed, she wouldn't be a whole lot better off, but at least she could cover the skimpy uniform with a blue sweater. She'd found the sweater in Miz Whitehead's trash bin — Miz Mayfield's neighbor. Miz Mayfield and Miz Whitehead were two of a kind, her Mama always said — too-rich-for-their-own-good white women who didn't have nothin' for nobody, 'specially no coloreds. "Only thing you can do with the likes of them," Mama would say, "would be to kill 'em with kindness. That's what Jesus would have you do." Mama had said that was what Lea's granddaddy would always do, and it worked for him. After he died, they even put a marker out for him, that said, "I treated those right who treated me wrong." Well, Lea did the best she could to honor her granddaddy's memory, but it sure was hard.

When she walked into that kitchen this morning, it would surely be a mess. Li'l Jenny Mayfield and her brother Billy were always comin' to the kitchen after dark and sneakin' sweets. Lea's Mama always made the Mayfields a big pound cake to last through the week, but it never made it past Wednesday. Them two young'uns would sneak into the darkness, get ahold of that cake, and that would be that. Their Mama never said a word. Sometimes they would drop cake crumbs all over the place, and ants would joyfully swarm with a vengeance. Lea had sprinkled boric acid in the corners of the kitchen, but rather than being discouraged by it, the little buggers seem to thrive on the stuff.

Her Mama would be home this weekend. It would be the first time in over a month that they had the same weekend off. Mama worked way 'cross the county at the Johnson house. She slept in six days one week, and then five the next. Annie Lee, Lea's older sister, took care of the other five while she and Mama worked. She missed them. She really did. "If there was any other way . . . ," her mama had said, shaking her head sadly. "If there was just another way. . . ."

But there wasn't. Lea was just about finished dressing,

and she looked over and saw the sun peeking through the trees. Two more years and she would be free. Mama had said it, so it must be true. She was bonded to the Mayfields till then, but after that . . .

Mama had told her how Papa used to be a sharecropper for Mister Mayfield, and how when Papa died, he still owed Mister Mayfield a good bit. There wasn't no money left over after the buryin', even after the Good Samaritans paid Mama her widow money, so how could Mama pay him off? Mister Mayfield, kind soul that he was (least to hear *him* tell it), agreed that four years of Lea's life would do just fine. That seemed quite fair, after all. Lea was the Mayfields' now, and there wasn't a thing nobody could do about it.

The kitchen was a mess; just like she expected it would be. Nobody was up yet, so Lea figured she would be able to steal a few moments of peace and quiet 'fore the start of another busy day.

"Lea!" Miz Mayfield called from her bedroom.

"Ma'am," Lea answered promptly. She walked over to the closed door and waited.

"We got company comin' Friday and stayin' till Sunday. That means you got extra work. You can't be goin' home this weekend — maybe next, we'll see. Meantime, go to the smokehouse and get two of them hams. You gonna need to get started soon if you gonna be ready. You hear me, Lea?"

"Yes, ma'am," Lea choked back a sob.

"You all right, Lea? You ain't' gettin' sick, are you? I got to have you at your best this weekend. You all right?"

"Yes, ma'am, I'm fine." Lea wiped the tears away. Tears

were for babies, and she sure wasn't nobody's baby. Maybe her daddy had been right when he said that sometimes happiness was a promise that reigned up in Heaven, a million miles away. Lea pulled her sweater closer around her. It wouldn't do much against the cold out there, but it was all she had, so she opened the door, braced herself, and made her way quickly to the smokehouse.

AFTERTHOUGHTS

Nursery rhymes. Soul-soothing lullabyes. Hand-clapping games. Silly, silly songs. Ring games. Hip shakes. Fairy tales.

These are the oral traditions of childhood, and to hear a particular favorite as an adult is to bring about fond memories of youth. Mothers rocked us to sleep with a lullabye. Daddies tickled our toes to some outrageous little beat, our friends pranced around us in ridiculous little ring games, and fairy tales were woven with hopes and dreams. The hidden message behind each was that someone would take care of us. Innocence of the harsh realities of life was an unspoken gift given free to all children.

Children lore is the scholarship of the childhood experience. Just as folklore is the passing on of wisdom and tradition from adult to adult, or from adult to child, children lore is the passing on of experience and tradition from child to child. For years, researchers in this field studied children lore from only one perspective — a Eurocentric one. They studied one body of childhood traditions and concluded that the cultural perspectives behind these creative expressions were the same for all children. Well, they are not, and they never have been.

Just as adults of different ethnic groups have created their own bounty of folklore to reflect their distinctive view of the world, so, too, have the children of these same groups. If we listen closely to the seemingly silly rituals and watch ever so carefully how little ones "play," we quickly realize that there is nothing short of genius here as the young interpret for us their environments, their experiences, their fears, their hopes, and their very dreams.

For the little colored child, life was more than tough — it was a cruel mockery of the promise that if you are good, then you will be happy. They heard that often enough on the lips of folks who tried and tried to get them to believe it, but they looked around them at their own reality and soon realized they'd be crazy to allow themselves to be fooled by such nonsense. None of the fairy princesses had kinky hair or full lips. None of the heroes were shades of pretty brown or deep, deep chocolate. None of the fairy godmothers looked like or worked as hard as their own mamas, scrubbing behind folks that didn't care nothing for them. Not one of the kings picked cotton like their daddies did till their fingers bled or their backs were breaking, and not one of the little children dressed in the rags that resembled their own clothing. They looked at the little shacks they called home and decided that no amount of pretend was going to turn them into castles and none of the silly songs or fancy dances had a thing to do with them, so they created their own body of children lore that was real and sounded good to them. It was theirs, and nobody could touch it.

Miss Sally Walker might have been a staple on the plantation for all antebellum children, but she was special for the slave children. She wasn't just some little girl shaking things around a bit; she was the white and weepy slave mistress whom they could poke fun at without her even knowing. Ring games have been around forever and are a significant part of "play" for all children, but watch the African American child and you'll notice that the dance is more of a sensual rhythm, the behind dips a bit lower, and the words are more improvised and sometimes even a bit naughtier.

The preceding stories were tough ones for me to create. My own childhood was a happy one, and I would like to think that the childhood of *my* children is very much the same. However, I have listened to many stories from folks now in their seventies and eighties who grew up in a segregated and impoverished South and never had a real childhood. Maybe some of the whimsical and spontaneous things they do now in their later years represent an attempt to make up for some of what they missed early on.

I listened with great admiration as they shared with me the sad experiences of leaving school in order to work and help support their families. I listened in horror as women shared with me a common experience of being abused by white men and how their parents were powerless to interfere. They cried as they told me how they had been made to feel ugly and unworthy because of their dark skin and unruly hair. They had wished time and time again for sweet blond curls and big blue eyes, as if that carried an assurance of happiness they couldn't get any other way.

Despite it all, however, they made it, and now as they nurture grandchildren and great-grandchildren, they can only hope that the world will finally deliver on childhood promises for happiness — at least for this generation of black babies. Still, they're not real sure about that. No, they really aren't very sure at all.

This series of three stories began with a nursery rhyme of my own creation. It is a rhyme dedicated to the survivors of those tough times and to the significance of their lives. It is not sweet. It is not pretty. It is not very joyous, but it certainly is real. As one man told me the stories of his painful childhood days, he said, "I don't reckon nobody will ever write about nothing like that. People don't want to write about a real colored childhood. They want to pretty it up so folks will feel good when they read it. Nope, ain't nobody gonna write about the real and the ugly." Well, he was wrong. Somebody has done just that, and I hope that I've done him and all the others the justice they deserve.

Willy Did It

Lil' Wilbert stood up and stretched. He'd been settin' on Miz Mildred's porch for near 'bout an hour and his behind had gone numb. He'd come just like she'd said for him to — right after school let out with no stoppin' 'long the way or takin' time to talk to nobody. His mama had said that Miz Mildred wanted to see him and he'd best not to keep her waiting. He was in trouble again, he just knew it. He didn't know what he'd done this time, but he knew trouble when he saw it. He'd seen it clear as day when he'd walked up and Miz Mildred hadn't even thought to hug him. She just looked at him with her arms stiffly folded, shook her head from side to side, and then pointed to the steps, silently telling him to sit. Then she'd just stomped on into the house to finish her supper without so much as a by-your-leave.

He could smell the fried chicken though, and it sho' smelled good. His stomach rumbled in appreciation and he patted it hard, warning it against making another sound. There probably wouldn't be any chicken in his future — well, least not today. Folks in trouble never got fed too good. He knew that on account of his big brother telling him so. When Elvin had gotten drunk and took to fighting with that no good Neckbone over some girl what hung out at Mister Sam's juke joint, the sheriff had hauled the two of 'em off to jail. He didn't give 'em nothing but cracklin' bread and syrup water for three whole days while they was sleeping it off and waiting to see if they would be joining up with the colored chain gang that would be putting in that new road at the far end of the town. The mayor was the one that decided them things. Mama had gone down there and talked to him though, and Mayor Frank had finally decided to let 'em both go.

Elvin had said that the waiting was the hardest. Not knowing how much trouble you was in, or what folks were going to do to you once they'd decided, could pluck on anybody's nerves. This waiting around for Miz Mildred was surely plucking his. Seemed like no matter what happened around this place, he seemed to get blamed for it. For as long as he could remember, everybody anywhere near has loved to utter them fateful words: "Willy did it."

It was his two older sisters' fault. Every time his mama would ask "Who?" with her lips drawn up tight, they would answer "Willy. Willy did it, Mama. He sho' did. Willy did it." It seemed like he'd been hearing it 'fore he could even talk good enough to defend himself. Fact was, he'd heard it so much when he was little that he figured that that must of been his name — Willy did it. Most folks had two names, he reckoned he just had three.

Willy did it. Willy did it. Willy did it. It was the national anthem in his house and everybody loved to sing along. Wasn't too long before his sisters had taken the message beyond the walls of their own home and started sharing it with the whole rest of the world. "Willy did it," they happily chanted when Pastor James asked who had snuck into the church storage room and drunk up all the communion wine. It didn't help none either that his tongue was still red. "Willy did it," they'd snickered when his mama asked who had been stupid enough to pull up all of her tomato plants instead of the weeds when tending to the vegetable garden. "Willy did it," they said as they pointed right to him when his daddy asked who'd tripped over his fishing bucket and forgot to pick it back up, settin' loose dozens of slimy little worms that were making their way slowly 'cross the back porch. Willy hadn't said one word, just looked down at the floor.

Willy did it. Willy did it. Willy did it. Bad part about the whole thing was that he got hisself into so much trouble it was hard to keep it all straight. Sometimes it got all mixed up in his head and then he couldn't remember whether he'd done it or not. Other times he got into trouble, and 'cause folks was so used to it nobody would even remember to tell him what he'd done — just skipped straight over the accusing part and went right to the punishing. So there come some times when he wasn't quite sure which punishment went with which deed.

Today he was in trouble with Miz Mildred and he didn't know what for — but one thing 'bout Miz Mildred, she didn't hop around a thing. If she had something on her mind, she would sho' 'nough let it fly. He didn't know what he'd done but he'd know soon enough, he was sure of it. He just hoped it wasn't something too bad. He was bound to get into trouble when his own folks discovered that he'd been the one that had spilled all that sugar all over the kitchen floor just last night. When he'd gotten up this morning there had been hundreds of ants all over the kitchen floor right up near to the back door. He'd grabbed him a piece of cornbread and a glass of buttermilk for breakfast and lit on out of there, heading straight to school before anybody had a chance to discover his latest transgression. Soon as he got home though, his whole family would be waiting on him and once again they would all get together and sing their favorite song — "Willy did it." It had been an accident, but that didn't matter. All that mattered was that Willy did it. Willy did it. Willy did it.

Lord have mercy, he wished Miz Mildred would come out. He'd rather get it over with. All this waiting was killing him and was always worse than the punishing. 'Course grown-ups knew all about that, that was why they put you through it. When his mama really wanted to get to him, she didn't do too much punishing herself. Instead she would sit him in the kitchen as they both waited on his daddy to get home from the fields, reminding him over and over again how mad he was gonna be when he found out what else Willy had done. He would just sit there as his mama went on and on, just imagining all the horrible things his daddy could do to him. By the time his mama had taken her time recounting his crimes for his daddy later that evening and his daddy had taken a moment of weary silence before telling him to go get the switch, then carefully examining the limb to make sure it had just enough sting, the beating was a downright relief. 'Course Willy had this thing down to a science.

You had to pick you a switch that had enough green and enough brown that it wouldn't hurt too much. All the brown ones broke almost as soon as they hit your legs. That was bound to make your daddy madder than the devil. He was sure to pick out the next one, and you could bet he'd pick out one of them really green ones that could go all night, if your daddy had a mind to. No, the trick was picking out one that was green with just a touch of brown around it. Them were the kind that after about four good hits was sure to give way and break right in half. His daddy was one of the nicer ones, so four good hits usually left him pretty satisfied, and if Willy put his mind to it he could get through four hits without too much agony. The trick was forcing yourself not to think about it whilst they was hitting. *After* the stick broke, then you had to remember to cry and cry just right. If you didn't cry right then, they'd beat you again 'cause they didn't think they'd done it right the first time. Cry too much and that would make folks mad too, and sometimes they took to yelling and threatening more. "Shut that noise up, boy, 'fore I give you something to really cry about," his grandma loved to say.

For an old lady, his grandma used to be able to really swing a switch. Now she was past her prime. Her legs bothered her and she couldn't get around too good, so he had to do all the punishing work for her now. First he'd have to tell her several times what he'd done 'cause she'd remember one minute but forget the next. He'd have to holler it too to make sure she heard it all, and then he'd have to go get the switch. Once he'd picked out the perfect one he had to help her position it in her one good hand, 'cause one hand didn't open and the other one did, but it was all twisted up so she had a hard time getting ahold of things. After that, he had to make sure he got close enough so she could reach him without having to swing too wide 'cause she had arthritis in her elbow. Once she'd hit him a couple of times he had to put on a real good show, pretending all the while that she'd hurt him with all that hitting when in reality she'd probably missed him altogether. Finally he had to hug her 'round the neck and tell her he was sorry and then help her into bed, 'cause all of that activity was sure to wear her out. He loved his grandma though. He usually tried real hard not to do anything too much to upset her. Sometimes he just couldn't help it, however.

Miz Mildred came out at last. She sat down in her chair and pointed for him to sit again. She didn't offer him one of her sitting chairs, so it was either the steps or the damp ground. He chose the steps.

"So, boy, what all you been up to?" She was chewing tobacco so it came out sounding all run together, but he understood. But what was he supposed to say? Was this some kind of trick to get him to tell something he wasn't ready to admit to yet, or was she just making conversation?

"Boy, you ever heard tell of Wiley and the Hairy Hairy Man?" She looked over at him real serious-like.

"Wiley? He got a name almost like mine," Willy said, proudly pointing out that he'd almost been made the star of a story.

"Well, he ain't you, so just hush up. 'Course, now his story could be your story if you don't start acting right.

That Hairy Hairy Man is all the time looking for them ones that's causin' a ruckus."

The Hairy Hairy Man, Willy thought. Ain't nobody ever told him about nothing like that, and Willy wasn't too sure he wanted to be hearing about it now. Didn't look like he had no choice in the matter though. Miz Mildred had already leaned back her chair into its famous storytelling position, and she'd spit the chewing tobacco out too. This was serious stuff. He'd better listen up.

"Now they tell me that Wiley's daddy was just no darn good. Fact was that he'd steal watermelons after dark, and one time he even robbed a dead man Joyner had laid out for burying. They even said that he was messing around with old man Hesse's new young bride, but chile, that's another story. So you see, everybody knew that when Wiley's daddy died he'd never cross Jordan 'cause the Hairy Hairy Man would sure 'nough be waiting for him. That must of been what happened, 'cause they never found him after he fell drunk face first into Crooked Creek that runs just a few miles from here. They looked for him everywhere but they ain't never found him, and when they heard a big man laughing 'cross the river, everybody just figured out that it was the Hairy Hairy Man and they stopped looking.

"'Wiley,' his mama told him, 'the Hairy Hairy Man done got your daddy and he's gonna get you too if you don't watch out.' 'Yes, Mama,' Wiley replied. 'I'll be sure to take my hound dogs everywhere I go.'

"Wiley knew that the Hairy Hairy Man didn't like no hound dogs 'cause his mama had told him and she knew stuff like that there. Why, she even knew conjure, that magic that gets folks to acting anyway you wants 'em to by

170

mixing this and that together just right. Well, Wiley's mama knew conjure, so of course, she knew all about a Hairy Hairy Man. Anyways, not too long after that, Wiley went out to cut some wood for his mama. He took his hound dog with him too, but soon as they got to where they was going, that hound dog saw a rabbit and took off to chasing him. Sho' 'nough, here come the Hairy Hairy Man.

"Lord have mercy, that Hairy Hairy Man was ugly as sin too. He was hairy all over, his eyes bugged out, and he had real big teeth. Well, Wiley got scared as could be and climbed up a real big tree. He knew that the Hairy Hairy Man couldn't come up there on account of them big cow feet he had. Do you know that that Hairy Hairy Man looked up at Wiley and said, 'You can't get away from me and I'm gonna get you too.' Then he picked up Wiley's ax and started chopping down the tree. Wiley was scared then, but soon after, his hound dog come on and chased that Hairy Hairy Man clear on outta there. When Wiley got home, he told his mama what happened.

"'Did he have his sack?' she asked him.

"'Yes, ma'am,' said Wiley.

"'Next time that he comes after you, don't climb up no tree. Just stay on the ground and say, "Hello, mister Hairy Hairy Man." You understand what I'm telling you?' she asked firmly. Well, Wiley understood, but for the life of him he couldn't figure out how just standing around saying hello was going to help somebody eye to eye with a Hairy Hairy Man.

"'He ain't gonna hurt you, chile,' she said. 'I knows. You can put him in the dirt and I'm gonna tell you how to do it.'

"'I don't know,' Wiley told her. 'If I just stand around,

he might just grab me and put me in that croaker sack he always has.'

"'You do like I says,' his mama said back. 'You says to him, "Hello, mister Hairy Hairy Man." Then you say, "Hairy Hairy Man, I done heard you the best conjure man around." Then he's gonna say, "I reckon I am." Then you gonna say, "I bet you can't turn yourself into no giraffe," and he will. Then you say, "Well, anybody can turn themselves into something as big as a man, but I bet you can't turn yourself into nothin' as small as a possum." Then he will, and that's when you grab him.' Well, Wiley figured his mama was pretty smart about these things, but still he wasn't sure about it all.

"So Wiley went out and tied up his hound dogs. He couldn't take them on account of the fact that he would scare away the Hairy Hairy Man. Then he went on down to the swamp and sure enough here he come along ugly as can be and grinning like always. He figured Wiley was gonna climb up that tree, but Wiley didn't do that. He did just like his mama told him and soon the Hairy Hairy Man turned himself into a giraffe and finally a possum and Wiley grabbed him just like his mama said to and threw him into the croaker sack. He took the sack down to the river and threw it in. He was heading home through the swamp, and who did he see but the Hairy Hairy Man looking down at him.

"'I turned myself into the wind and blew myself right out of the sack,' the Hairy Hairy Man told him. Oh no, Wiley was in for now. The Hairy Hairy Man was gonna get him and there was nobody around to stop him. His hound dogs were all tied up. Wiley figured he'd try to trick that

172

Hairy Hairy Man one more time, so he looked at him and said, 'I'll bet you can't make things disappear.' The Hairy Hairy Man said, 'I bet I can,' so Wiley challenged him to make a tree disappear and he did. Then Wiley asked him if he could make all the rope in the world disappear, including the magic rope holding up his britches, and he did that too. Well, Wiley figured if the rope holding up his pants was gone, then the rope tying up his dogs was gone too, so he called them. 'Here boy, here boy,' and they come running up and chased that Hairy Hairy Man right away.

"When Wiley got home he told his mama what happened. 'That's bad,' she said, 'but you done got away twice. You fool him once more and he'll leave you alone for good.'

"'Well,' said Wiley, 'then you gots to figure out a way to fool him.'

"'Okay,' said his mama. 'I'll think one up and let you know.' She sat down by the fire with her head in her hands and started studying things real hard. Wiley wasn't studying nothing though but keeping that Hairy Hairy Man away. So while his mama was studying, he did all the things he knew to scare away evil. He took his hound dogs out and tied one to the front porch and one to the back and then he used an ax handle and an old broomstick and made a cross over the front door. Finally he made a fire in the fireplace and then sat down next to his mama. After a while she said to go on down to the pigpen and get that baby pig. 'Bring it here. After that you go on up to that loft and hide.'

"Wiley did what she told him to. After a while he heard the wind howling and the trees blowing and the dogs barking. He looked out through a knothole and saw something ugly comin' from the direction of the swamp and heading to their front door. 'Lordy,' said Wiley, 'the Hairy Hairy Man is coming for sure.' He heard something like a cow running and he knew the Hairy Hairy Man was there. Then he heard a knock on the front door, big as you please.

"'Mama,' said the Hairy Hairy Man, like he had a mama. 'Mama,' he said again, 'I done come for your baby.'

"'You can't have him,' said Wiley's mama.

"'You give him to me or I'll conjure you,' said the Hairy Hairy Man.

"'I know conjure too,' said Wiley's mama, 'and I ain't afraid of you.'

"'You give me that baby or I'll set your house afire.'

"'That would be pretty mean,' said Wiley's mama.

"'That's 'cause I is mean,' he said.

"'Well,' said Mama, 'if I give you my baby, will you promise to go away and never ever come back?'

"'Yeah,' said the Hairy Hairy Man.

"'Well,' said Mama, 'he's over there in that bed.'

"Well, the Hairy Hairy Man walked over to the bed and snatched back the covers. 'Hey,' he said, 'there ain't nothing here but a pig.'

"'I ain't said what kind of baby I was going to give you. That there is my baby too, or least it was 'til I give him to you.' Now the Hairy Hairy Man was too mad then. He stomped and screamed awhile 'fore he picked up that pig and left. The next day the swamp looked like it had been lifted up and slashed straight through the middle. The trees were torn out from the roots and there was rocks everywhere. Wiley figured that it was finally okay to come down from his hiding place.

"'Is everything all right, Mama?' he asked.

"'Yep,' said Mama, 'we done fooled him three times. He's gone for good. You ain't got to worry. But I tell you this, Wiley, and you tells everybody you know that if you're no count, do no good, sass grown folks, or treat people evil then the Hairy Hairy Man is gonna come get you just like he come for your daddy, and chile, not even their mama gonna be able to save them then.'

"Well, Willy grew up to be a fine young man and he never did nobody wrong 'cause he always remembered what his mama said, and he declared to everybody that anytime he even thought about being bad he would see the Hairy Hairy Man grinning over his head."

At the end of the story, Miz Mildred looked at him for a minute and then waved him on his way. The Hairy Hairy Man. Now he had something else to worry about. Wasn't it enough that he spent all that time and energy trying so hard to be good, now he had to worry on a monster too. Jeez, Willy thought grudgingly, an eight-year-old just didn't stand a chance.

AFTERTHOUGHTS

The power of the front porch has always been a significant part of African American heritage. It was especially significant in the socialization of black children. Dr. Spock was not a part of my grandmother's reality, so the raising up of a child into the way it should go would have come from tried-and-true, old-fashioned methods — Bible stories sometimes and folktales the other. The antics of Brer Rabbit could take on the same serious implications as the disciples themselves if the telling of the story was done just right. Listen to Anasis the spider, the old folks would say, and you could find all the wisdom that you were looking for. Folklore provided proverbial paths to good living, and the listener best heed all the appropriate warnings.

Rural African Americans often used a tale of some other equally frightening possibility to scare children into proper behavior. Sass an elder in the church and their spirit was likely to haunt you for the rest of your days. Naughty at school? Watch out for the pig lady 'cause she was sure to be waiting, anxious to carry you off to a place where nobody would ever hear from you again. Staying out late at night? Beware the night doctors — those white medical men who roamed the black side of town looking for the useless and disobedient to drag back to their labs to experiment on. "That's how come they know so much," folks would say, "'cause they all the time a-cutting us up and peeking inside, learning what all they needs to." Even during slavery the superstitious nature of the black folks themselves was often used against them as masters created tales about the frightening possibilities of escape. The human patrollers were one thing, but the ghosties who loved to eat up runaway slaves was another.

"Wiley and the Hairy Hairy Man" is an old African American tale that has existed for generations. I love to hear it and I love even better telling it. I use stories to socialize my own children — biblical ones as well as the longstanding cultural variety. I try to emphasize the lesson within the story rather than the more frightening aspects, hoping they get all the same wonderful wisdom I received when I first heard it. If any of you ever get tired of running yourselves crazy with all this newfangled stuff on child rearing, there's always the old-fashioned way, and I have plenty of good stories to share with you that I guarantee will work just fine.

White Folks

White Folks

White folks. In all my born days, the white folks in this town done only come two ways — quality white folks and poor white trash. Now, them two right there is really 'bout different as collards and cabbage, though some folks would call 'em both greens. 'Course don't neither of them there white folks mean us coloreds one bit of good. Mama used to say that "there ain't much difference between a hornet and a yellowjacket when they gets up in your britches, and baby, either of 'em will tear up your tail if you don't get him 'fore he gets you!"

Now, your poor white trash can be some mean, hate-filled son-of-a-gun. Sometimes they hate gets so big that it can't even rightly stay inside 'em, then it gets to walkin' on beside 'em and whisperin' a whole lot of mess — and we all in trouble then! That's why they can't keep the right and wrong straightened out, you see — they too busy listenin' to all them evil spirits. If they would just be still and get kinda quiet, they would hear for theyselves the voice of the

Lord. And then they would know we don't mean 'em one bit of harm.

But that poor white trashy man ain't listenin' for no goodness — he's too busy bein' meaner than a junkyard dog. He ain't got nothin', and he's surrounded by nothin' — but still, what little he sees is supposed to be his, and he can get to barkin' pretty loud if he thinks anybody is fixin' to get anywhere near it. 'Course your colored man is every bit as down and out as that white man — sometimes worser — and there gonna come times when there ain't gonna be but one stingy little bone to go on round.

Now what you got? I'll tell you what — two hungry, down-and-out dogs with they eye on the same bone. Yeah, that's 'bout the way it is with us coloreds and them poor white folks — we's a-wallowing in the exact same trash, but ain't neither of us got sense enough to realize that the fight ain't with one another, it's really 'bout them others.

Now we done arrived at them quality white folks I was telling you about. Them the ones that got every dang-blasted thing you can think of, and they aiming to keep it that way too! They ain't lookin' to give none of it to no coloreds, and they ain't got nothin' much for them poor white folks, neither, even though they got them fooled into thinkin' that they do. 'Long as they can keep 'em down there wallowing in all that trash, and a-fightin' with us over them same couple of bones, then them poor ones won't have to come after them — you know, the quality white folks. See, if us coloreds and them down-and-out white folks would ever get together, then we'd be plenty strong enough to take all we needed. It ain't never gonna happen, though, 'cause they been taught too long and too strong that we the ones they got to hate to make it, and you can't sense 'em into nothin' else.

Now your quality white folks, they is the tricky sort, I do declare. They don't act up like them others, nosirree, 'cause they ain't got to. They just don't say nothin' — nothin' at all. They figure we supposed to be smart enough to know that we wouldn't know what in the world to do without 'em. Now, them kind ain't got to be a-barkin' and a-howlin' — a dog only needs do that when he's scared, and them there know they ain't got nothin' to fear from us. We ain't no threat, no threat at all. I can tell you this, though — they might not fear us, but they sho' as the dickens need us. We got to do everything for 'em 'cause they sho' can't take care of theyselves. Miss Anne, the lady I worked for, she couldn't iron, wash, cook, or take care of her own babies. Now, what kind of woman is that?

Well, them quality white folks, like I said, they is somethin' else. They can look right at us, but 'lessen they needs us for a thing, well, they don't even bother to see us. I remember one time when I was out a-wandering, I seen her, Miz Anne, coming on down my way. She looked right at me, and believe it or not, she still ain't seen me. Why should she? At that moment she didn't need no wash-woman, wasn't lookin' for no nursemaid, and couldn't use no beast to bear none of her burdens. So since she ain't need me, well, I just ceased to be. What a sight she was, all dressed up in her finery, but finer ain't never meant better. Yeah, my skirt was soiled with them years of hard work and toil, but hers was tainted, too — stained with all my blood, my sweat, and my tears. There we were, her womanhood and my womanhood, just a-standin' there so very close but yet so far apart.

Them mens may be fightin' over the same old bones for a long time to come. You can't really blame 'em, neither — it's all they have ever knowed. No, it will take my sister and me to join hands and reach for that miracle together if it's ever gonna be. We bring the world its babies, and we ought to have an understandin' that a man will never know — but chile, it's sad to say, it still ain't so. I'm just a sister away from my healin', but my partner, well, she just plain refuses to see it.

I wonder when they said the black woman was the mule of the Earth, did they say it 'cause they knew they had burdened us with something no other soul would dare try to carry?

Did they know we were too strong to be crushed under the weight of affliction, or did they finally realize that we were too stubborn not to make it all the way through?

Why can't she see that this headrag is not a banner of surrender but my crowning glory, and these scars are not welts of weakness but the punctuation marks of a well-fought war story?

Oh, why must my fair sisters be the other woman? Don't they know that we, too, have been all that they have been — saint, sinner, priestess, and madonna? Can't they look past the depths of our destitution and see all the glory, or are they afraid to see a reflection of what could someday be their own story? After all, ain't we women, too?

White folks. Poor white trash and them quality ones, too. They sure is some funny folks. They figure this world will be just fine if we do just what they want us to and stay where they tell us to. 'Long as we can stay on out of they way, well, maybe, just maybe, they might let us be. But I got to ask you, what's gonna happen round here when we get sick of bein' told and fed up with bein' put? What's gonna happen when we colored women gets tired of bein' somebody's nursemaid and our men get tired of bein' everybody's nigger? I just got to ask you, what in the world you figure gonna happen then?

Hagar's Children

Bless Gracious! I reckon I been settin' out here thinkin' since the sun bid me good day more than a few hours ago — but then I been remembering, too. You know there sure is somethin' mighty special 'bout this here peculiar bit of night that comes along right 'fore daylight. It's amazin' how a pretty little piece of quiet and some calming beauty of blackness can set an old body still and put a good mind to recollectin'. Now 'course all of my rememberings ain't so good — I got me some rememberings that run so deep till they live here in the pit of my stomach and touch the center of my very soul. It's one of them there that I been settin' here studyin' on. . . .

It was one of them yesterdays that the Lord was fixin' up to be something wonderful. It introduced itself onto that early-morning sky in a burst of absolute glory. Then the Devil came along. He decided he couldn't just let it be, so he stuck his hands into the mixin' and the makin's of it. 'Fore you knew a thing he had stirred up stuff pretty bad.

All of a sudden that warm wonderful goodness was clean gone away, and there was nothin' but a cold hard day a-starin' back at me. A day when I would live through the kind of pain that washes over the body like bloodstained rains. A day when Hagar's children would decide they deserved a place next to Sarah's precious babies. A day when hell would rise up from underneath the Earth's floor and come a-knockin' right up to my front door. A day that as long as I live, I won't ever forget.

I remember 'cause even though it was one of them beautiful springtime dawns, there was no plowing in the fields and no hustle and bustle humming about. Nope — nothin'. My husband, looking 'bout poor as Job's turkey, come a-stumbling up the walkway wearin' that felt hat of his slung way down low on 'cross his big head — but I could still see his eyes, and they was clouded with misery and sorrow. He rested hisself right down next to me, and we sat there on them rickety porch steps for almost ten whole minutes 'fore either of us said one single word. Then he told me. Just blurted it straight out — but I knew it even 'fore he said it. Knew it 'fore that barnyard owl screeched right in my left ear. Knew it 'fore the March winds blew the smell of death right up near. I knew it sho' 'nough 'cause the spirit had already showed it to me a long time ago.

"Me and Bo went out there early this morning like you said for us to. It was like you pictured it — but hell, it was even worse than you seen it." He stopped talkin' for a bit and grabbed hold of my hand. "Richard was layin' in that little ditch that runs on 'cross their back door. They must have tied him to somethin' or 'nother and then dragged him throughout that entire place, 'cause when we found him he was facedown in the dirt but the back of his head was clean gone away, and his brains had oozed on down to the back of his shirt. They ain't killed Sister Nora right off — maybe they showed her some mercy and spared her some on account of that baby she was carryin'. They beat her somethin' awful, though — her eyes were so swollen shut that we had to tell her three times who we was 'fore we was able to sense it into her and she could get it clear through."

He stopped for a minute. Maybe it was to catch his breath 'cause he been spilling that there faster than a preacher pocketing pennies. Maybe it was just to choke back some of the pain or swallow him back some of that rage. I don't rightly know 'cause I ain't looked at him. I couldn't. Just kept starin' straight ahead like there was something magical out there in front of me that would take all the pain away.

"Did she say anything to you?" At least I managed to spit that much out, but it wasn't easy 'cause my gut was risin' up fast to meet the back of my throat.

"Yeah, yeah, she did. She begged me to save that baby of hers — asked me to birth it right then and there and take it over to Suda Mae's so she could raise it on up in the way it should go."

He stopped again. This time I knew it 'cause he was sobbin'. I could feel his teardrops hittin' the back of my hand that was restin' inside his. But I knew he didn't want me to know he was a settin' there boohooing like somebody's newborn babe, so I still ain't looked at him. Just kept a-starin' straight ahead, waiting on that miracle to come.

"Now, I ain't got me no kinda understandin' 'bout birthin' no babies." He told it to me like I ain't already know. "I done helped a few horses in my day, but that's really 'bout all. 'Course I knew if it was left up to me to save that chile's blessin', then me and the Savior would stumble on through and do it just like we manages to do everything else we do. I was prayin', somethin' powerful, that I might still have me a li'l more time, so I sent Bo on out to fetch Bertha the medicine woman."

My eyes were closed then — at least I think they was; they might've just been bustin' full of heartache. I knew he was lookin' at me. I could just feel it, could feel that exact moment he turned his love to me. I opened up my mouth and tried to say somethin', anything, but wouldn't nothin' come loose, so I just sat there with my lips locked up together tight. I knew he didn't want to tell me no more — some things just ain't fit to be throwed up on no man, woman, or chile — but Hagar's babies are built to shoulder some mighty big loads, and I wasn't 'bout to let nobody carry mine.

"I sat there holdin' her. I knew you wouldn't mind me huggin' her a bit. I guess I was just hopin' that somehow, some of my strength would pass from outta me and into her. Maybe if I could just hold her long enough and strong enough, I would save her. But I reckon I ain't held on to her close enough, 'cause she didn't linger on me long — just ceased right there in my arms. Lord, it seem like no matter how hard we tries, us colored men just can't seem to hold our women close enough, long enough, or strong enough to keep some of hardship's dirt from landin' on 'em." Then he let out a long, long sigh — one of them

189

dredged-up-from-the-bottom-of-damnation kinds of sighs that only a colored man could bring on round.

"Bertha and Bo come up, then. We knew Sister Nora was gone, but that baby was movin' so till we could see it clear through all of her clothes. Bertha figured she could save it, had her mind set to savin' it, and went right at savin' it — but by the time she got Nora propped up like she was supposed to be, that baby was already slowin' down on his livin'. Bertha kept tryin', pushin' and a-pullin', tuggin' and a-reachin', but that baby wouldn't budge, not even one little bit. After awhile Bertha had to give it up 'cause she knowed it just won't gonna let go. So we all just stood there feeling 'bout helpless as could be and watched the life drain right on out of 'em. In a few minutes, well, he was gone, too. Lord, 'fore that young'un even had a chance at some livin', he had already been trialed, blamed, and executed."

"What y'all do then?"

"Well, we all knows how proud them two could be — they wouldn't had wanted nobody lookin' down at 'em with all their sufferin' hangin' clear out there in the open for all the world to see. So Bertha got 'em ready, and Bo and me, well, we buried 'em. We couldn't put 'em away without so much as a marker to remember 'em, so we cut the headboard off that bed Richard made the day they was married, and we used it to rest they heads. I reckon they in glory now, and a mite better off than them they left behind."

He was 'bout finished. I could always tell when he was comin' to the end of an especially hard row. "Yeah, baby, it

190

was just like you said it would be. The ways of some pretty evil white folks got ahold of 'em and carried 'em right on out of here. Sometimes I reckon that this here old world just ain't no place a colored soul ought to be." Then he stood up, walked off, and left me alone with my misery.

Sara's Precious Babies

She was suddenly awake. Normally when she was in a sound sleep, she didn't hear him when he returned, but today it was like the evil of the deed had its own presence and shook her right where she lay. It had been done. It was the same after any kill, whether it be a troublesome deer or a pesky nigger — he always skipped across the front yard in triumph. This time he wasn't alone — there was a second set of footsteps dragging on behind them first skipping ones, and now, as they entered her home, she could hear the muffled sounds of hushed voices and the sinister glee of softer laughter.

No matter how many times it happened, she was never quite ready for it — not even this time, when instead of being a spontaneous act, it had been carefully planned and executed. They'd even had the courtesy this time to warn her beforehand. She'd already seen it coming, though, way before the time of reckoning, and even before they had their usual "Darling, something has happened, and we have to handle it" talk. She had known it when Nora and Richard first came. They rode into town like they were something else, like they was already looking for some higher bushes and sweeter berries than all the rest of them others. Sitting so high and mighty — *her* back was way too straight, *his* eyes just too alert, *their* speech far too educated and certainly way too direct. Why, they didn't even lower their eyes when they talked to a white person. Wasn't no nigger born with a right to act like that — 'least, that was what Lester had told her. They wouldn't make it six months in this town, Lester had said again and again, and he was right — they hadn't even made it three.

That fool was probably out there right now dripping blood all over her freshly scrubbed floors and sloshing the celebratory moonshine all over her new tablecloth. It sounded like it was Mister Robert that was out there with him. Shameful. How could he be seen with that man, especially now that it was daylight and all? Everybody knew that he wasn't nothin' but poor white trash, but Lester insisted on him. Said nobody could string up a nigger better than Robert. Said watching him was like being in the presence of greatness. Lester said it was almost beautiful to see, except the niggers always managed to spoil it by not having the dignity to die gracefully. Lester said that they would usually beg for their lives so pitifully, and then their black faces would get all shiny with tears and sweat. And even as they were dying, when the course had been set and it was obvious that there wasn't but one way it would end, still they pleaded and they prayed, sometimes until their voices cracked, their eyes bulged, and their tongues hung limp and lifeless from their mouths. Usually — but not always. She certainly couldn't picture Nora like that, not with her face so much like that of a pretty brown angel and her head always pointed to the heavens somewhere. No, she sure couldn't picture Nora like that.

She felt queasy this morning. This was the first time in a long time that these things had made her sick to her stomach. She hadn't been this sick since the very first one so long, long ago, and Lester had told her then that if she was going to retch every time, she'd have no guts left by the time she was forty. So she'd grown up quickly and learned that none of it had one thing to do with her. She still couldn't stand it, but it was not her place to say anything — no, nothing at all. Her mama always said that as long as Lester was beating on the niggers, then maybe, just maybe, he wouldn't beat up on her.

Today, though, she wasn't just queasy, she was sad, too, and despite her will, the tears rolled freely down her cheeks. She sobbed as silently as she could, but she couldn't seem to stop it completely. Lord, if Lester heard her crying right now, he'd be hotter than piss in a July ditch. But today she could no more hold back the pain and sorrow than the morning sun could hold back the daylight. It just seemed to be busting out of her like the Lord had somehow sent it to her special. Well, then, it would just have to be. It wasn't that she especially liked Nora. She didn't know her well enough to like her or dislike her, but she did know that wasn't no nigger woman supposed to be that pretty. Still, she had to admit that she did like having Nora around. She could sew like a dream and made sweet-potato pies so good that they made you want to slap your brains out — but Lester hated her. She knew the reason that he hated Nora was that he wanted her — wanted her even when she was swollen with another nigger's leavings. He knew, too, that she was not his for the taking, so he hated her. And Nora, God rest her soul, let 'em all know she wasn't about to be no white man's whore.

She wasn't sure if she would miss Nora herself, but she was sure that she would miss her smile and her sweet-potato pies. Lord, surely she hadn't deserved this. Surely not. Not that some of 'em didn't deserve it, now. Why, one time she'd had this nigger woman make her a dress for her daddy's birthday party, and she'd told her three times that she wanted the pearls across the bodice and on down the sleeves. Well, that stupid nigger only remembered to put 'em on the bodice. Ruined her dress and her good time — now, *that* nigger should've been shot where she stood, but she was still walking on round here proud as you please. But Nora, who sewed like a dream and who had the face of an angel, was gone, never to be nowhere again — just 'cause she wouldn't be no man's whore.

Lester had him a nigger woman once. He thought she didn't know about her, but he was wrong. She'd always known, right from the first. She'd followed him one day to see which woman's scent it was that he had the nerve to bring to her bed. She'd thought it was Miss Melanie, the pretty blonde who ran the town store, but it wasn't Miss Melanie. It was a beautiful nigger wench who lived clear 'cross town. Even in her rags, she was so beautiful that she could steal your breath clear away. There was no love or joy in that woman's eyes as she stood on her shanty steps and watched Lester come to her — just a silent resignation. It was probably that very same look I have in my eyes when he comes to me, Sue thought, and she laughed bitterly. At first she'd thought that the nigger was nothin' more than a two-dollar whore, 'cause he'd pressed a handful of dollars into her hands as soon as he got near enough, but then a little boy came out the front door, and gracious sakes, he was the chocolate image of Lester! Right after, a little girl come along who didn't so much look like Lester, but she had her a white daddy for sure. Lester might hate them niggers in his heart, she thought, but that hatred sure don't reach down to that lower part of his body, the part he thinks with. She laughed again, even more bitterly this time.

She slid deeper into the covers and relished the few minutes of peace and quiet — he'd be calling her soon, she was sure of it. If only she could have said something to stop it — but what? Well, it didn't much matter, because he wouldn't have listened no way. If only she could leave — but go where? Living with her mama and daddy wasn't a possibility, and besides, she was sick of them anyway. She stood up quietly, walked over to the water basin, and washed the sleep and sorrow out of her eyes. She shivered. There seemed to be a chill in the room that went straight to the bone. Out of the window she could see dark and somber clouds sliding across the dreary sky. It was going to storm for sure. Maybe the rains would wash this day clean — it had a definite stench to it that was really quite offensive. Yes, let the rains come and wash the day clear.

There was a knock at the door. Lester. "Honey, you up? Sue, do you hear me?" Well, she might as well answer, 'cause even if she didn't, he wouldn't go away. He'd just bust on in like a bat out of hell.

"Yeah, I'm up," she answered. The door opened slowly, and Lester came in holding a bundle of soiled and bloody garments. "Oh, by the way, something happened, but we done already took care of it. I didn't wake you 'cause you was sleeping so soundly, but don't you worry, we done took care of it," and with that he slammed the door behind him. Worry? What should she worry 'bout something that wasn't even hers?

The dumb fool had flung them bloody clothes right on the floor — couldn't even walk the extra three feet needed to put 'em into the sink. Now look at that bloody puddle in the middle of her beautiful oak floors. It was raining pretty hard now, and the drops seemed to drum the despair of the day right smack into her head. She picked up the clothes and threw them into the sink. She grabbed her hammer off the fireplace. A hammer was one of her favorite things — one part could put stuff together, and the other part could rip it all apart again. Deadly but useful, kind of like some folks walking around her every day. She took a good strong swing with the pointed end, and it locked itself firmly into the floorboard. She tried to lift the plank clear out, but it wouldn't even budge. She freed her hammer and then tried it again. Oh, it was going to be a stubborn little devil, but no matter what, it had to go. The last time Lester had come in skipping, he'd skipped blood all over her front room. In her ignorance, she'd attempted to scrub away the ugliness — but even after she washed it clean, the blood would come again and again. Every single time it rained, the crimson pools would raise up from the dead, like Christ come a-calling to shake His finger at them. Finally she'd told Lester that the floor would just have to go. She slammed her hammer into the plank once more — sometimes it just wasn't enough to remove the sin, sometimes you simply had to destroy the carrier.

And the People of a Town Go Round and Round

Sue simply wasn't having a good morning. So far nothing was going right. Lester had told her he wanted roast chicken for supper and something *special* for dessert. Nothing in particular, just make it *special*. She'd already been to three different places, and one had a *pretty good* and two had OKs, but nobody seemed to have *special*. She could look in two more places and check with a few more folks, but *special* was looking like it was going to be hard to come by today.

It was the first day in a while that Main Street was good and crowded. It was nice to see all the usual folks milling around. It was also the first day since, well, you know, *it*. She'd been kind of reluctant to venture out so soon after and walk among the darkies, 'cause sometimes after one of these, you know, *unfortunate situations*, well, them folks just weren't that pleasant to be around. Not that they would step out of line, or get too surly, Lester made sure of that, but still they could be, well, you know, *different*. But today, though they were quieter then usual, and certainly more huddled together, they didn't seem to be so very different, and that was a blessing. Lord, if Nora was here, she would go pick up one of those wonderful sweet-potato pies. But Nora was gone, never to be nowhere again. Now what was she supposed to do, and where was she supposed to find *special?*

It sure was a pretty morning. The first clear day after a whole week of stormy ones. Lester looked on round at his town and everything seemed to be just fine — except for maybe one thing. He looked across Main Street again at the nigger sitting on the crate. Couldn't rightly figure out what in the world he could be up to. Not that he was doing anything unusual, mind you — still, just seeing him sitting there was mighty disturbing. The only reason somebody would be setting there like that was if they was waiting on the *Thunderbird* to come a-huffing and puffing on 'cross the horizon. Well, hell, if he was watching for that one, he'd have him a long wait. The railway had sent word that the train would be two hours late today.

That sure did look to be Clara's oldest boy sitting there. Jeez, he hadn't seen that old auntie in many a moon. He'd make it a point to find out where she'd been hiding herself lately. Still, that looked like her boy, all right, and he sure as hell was waiting on something or the other. He didn't have no bag or nothing. Didn't appear to be taking no trip, but who could figure a nigger? Lester could feel the hairs on the back of his neck begin to stand on end. Something wasn't right, and he was sure as hell determined to find out what it was.

Today Absalom Alexander Adams waited on salvation — *Absalom* 'cause his mama had read it in a Bible somewhere; *Alexander* so the white folks would think he had more proper in him than he really did; and *Adams* so the colored folks would know that he did indeed have him a daddy somewhere. But today didn't none of that matter. Today the stench of sin clung to him like the stinking smell of leftover Sunday cabbage on a beautiful and bright Monday morning. Yesterday his heart had belonged to the Savior, but today it had been sold to the Devil. Yesterday he had not known the power of hatred and vengeance, but today he had seen the depths of hell.

He looked out into the vastness and fiercely hoped that deliverance would soon be coming up over those hills, but all that danced before him was the evil of the deeds, first theirs and now his. Nora and Richard, with their loving hearts, had been eliminated with no more thought than most people would give to putting out the trash. Shameful. Simply shameful. Everybody knew that there was no law here for the coloreds, so Absalom had used one that had been around for ages — an eye for an eye. Yesterday he had not known what he was capable of, but today he knew. An eye for an eye. The Good Book had sanctioned it, and he had done exactly that.

They would know what he had done soon enough. They would come looking for him, but by then he would be long gone. If they asked his mama, and he was certain they would, she wouldn't tell them nothing 'cause she wouldn't know nothing. They might even smack her up a bit, but not too much. She had been Mister Lester's mammy, and she reminded him always that she was the mama that suckled him at her tit.

He hoped his mama would understand. She would know of his wrongdoings sure enough. She would have nowhere else to go and no one else to turn to, so she would do what she'd always done — she would pray for him. She would drop to her knees wherever she was and pray a prayer that could absolve Satan himself. Then she would weep for him. The tears would fill her eyes to the brim, but she would never allow them to fall. Mama allowed herself her moments of sorrow, but she never allowed them to overwhelm her. After the grieving was done, she would sing for him — sing one of those songs that could shake pain free from a hurting soul. Then she would rise and lift her hands up to the only Father she had ever known, and give her burden over to Him. She would know then that even if she never saw her boy again, things would be better by and by. The Father would make sure of it.

But Absalom had no father he could turn to — heavenly or otherwise. He had seen his daddy all of one day in his entire life. He tracked him to a prison camp about sixty miles north of here. He had peeked through the barbed-wire fences and watched the sweat roll off his daddy's back as he worked off his transgressions under the hot and blazing sun. A guard had finally spotted Absalom — a puffed-up white man who gave new meaning to the term "redneck." He had a toothpick in his mouth and a rifle by his side.

"What you want, boy?" the redneck asked.

"Just a chance to meet my daddy, sir," Absalom had pleaded.

"Which one is he?" the talking tomato asked.

"Jefferson Adams," the little boy had answered.

"Wait a minute and I'll get him," the talking tomato promised. And then he spit some snuff juice in a stream so long it would have made Miss Ruth proud, and folks said she was the champ!

"You got five minutes, you hear?"

"Yes, sir, I hear."

And so Absalom Alexander Adams had five minutes to learn and love his daddy, and the experience would have to last a lifetime. Not much had been said, but maybe there just hadn't been anything much to say. His daddy had looked at him and called him "Son." Then he'd smiled and told him to stay out of trouble, take care of his mama, and always, always stand up for himself like a man. "It won't be easy, boy, being a man in a place that don't seem to have much use for a strong colored man, but you be a man anyhow. You hear me, Son? You be a man." And then Absalom had watched his father walk out of his life forever. Well, he had taken good care of his mama, and yesterday he had proved himself a man. He hadn't been able to stay out of trouble, though, so two out of three would just have to be good enough. Sometimes a man had to raise a little hell and take a few prisoners.

The train was still nowhere to be seen. If it didn't get here soon, it would be too late. Too late for a second chance. Too late for saving grace. Absalom wondered if they caught him what he would feel as they slipped the noose around his neck. Would he feel fear, or would that be his final chance to be a man? He wondered if death would come all at once, or creep through his body slowly like a good drunken high? He wondered what hell would be like, and how many devils he would already know when he got there.

Absalom could still see Richard and Nora lying there bloodied and brutalized. He hadn't actually seen them, but Bo had painted him a pretty detailed and gruesome picture. Well, he had not been able to save them, but he had sure as the dickens avenged them. Justice had been served on their behalf, and they could rest easy now.

The *Thunderbird* shimalackied to a complete halt without fuss or circumstance. It was a matter of course — a course that had been set and had remained for a hundred years or more. The locomotive always pulled in, waited exactly twenty minutes so the passengers could get on board or off, and then pulled off once again. Walter Johnson had been the conductor for almost forty years, and rarely did he have to utter one sound. Everyone knew what to do and where to go. It was an amazing thing, this thing we called life, he thought. His daddy had called it right when he said that the more things change, the more things stay the same, especially in this here town.

Eighteen minutes, almost time to go. Walter looked outside to make sure that all was clear. The nigger on the crate was nowhere to be seen; must've already made his way down to the freight car. Lester was across the way leaning on his favorite post, watching the makings of his town and tapping nervously to his own inner beat. Walter noticed the colored couple that were making their way slowly 'cross Main Street. They had been with him since Jackson, Mississippi, and now it looked like they had finally reached their destination.

For coloreds they seemed like a handsome pair. The man was tall, jet-black, with fine features and even white teeth. He spoke in a cultured voice and sang in an amazing baritone. Walter had had a chance to hear him sing just hours ago when he was checking up on the passengers in the back. The wife was an absolute beauty. With her head held high and her graceful swinging hips, she looked like one of them African queens.

Walter looked at the colored couple, then at Lester, and then back again at the couple. Seemed to him like he had dropped off another set just like 'em only a few months ago. He wondered what had happened to them. The wife made the best sweet-potato pie he ever had. She gave him a piece when she and her husband rode on his train. He hadn't had none so good before or since. They'd seemed anxious to get started here, and they had stepped off the train with vigor and gusto. Seemed like real nice people for coloreds. He wondered how they were doing.

Twenty minutes — time to go. He looked around once more to make sure all was clear. One thing about this town, didn't much seem to change here. Each trip was exactly alike. The coloreds huddled together near the number-running joint, and Lester stood on his corner. The couple were now making their way past Lester. Lester was looking the woman over carefully. He had a dangerous gleam in his eye. Walter had seen that look before. He pulled in the step-stool and signaled the engineer that it was time to go. Ain't it amazing, Walter thought, how the people of a town can just go round and round?

AFTERTHOUGHTS

I knew as soon as I decided to write *Just Plain Folks* that in order to show a full range of African American experiences, I had to do some stories about the bitterness and the brutality of racism as it existed in the South, from the Reconstruction era right up to the Civil Rights movement. I knew it wasn't going to be easy to deal with, but it turned out to be even more difficult to write than I had originally thought. I was doing fine until I began to write the story called "Hagar's Children." It was then that all hell broke loose. Because this entire story was completely created from my own imagination (it is not a rewritten version of an actual incident), I had to dredge up these characters from the depths of my heart and soul. In order to tell the tale the way it needed to be told, I had to feel my characters' pain as if it were my own.

I had to live through the entire experience. There were times during the writing when tears just streamed down my cheeks, and I realized then that I was crying not only for my characters but for real African Americans who had experienced these same kinds of tragedies, so prevalent in the South.

Vigilantism has historically taken on several different forms, depending on the purposes of the perpetrators. Ku Klux Klansmen flogged or made threatening visits to their victims with the intent of intimidating or terrorizing them; sometimes they burned crosses or serenaded them with ominous music. Lynch mobs, in contrast, came solely to kill. They killed *their* victims with cowardice, without conscience, and usually without consequence. Not until 1982 were efforts made to gather data on lynchings across the United States. During the sixty-year period from 1892 to 1950, over six thousand blacks were executed. Very few participants in lynch mobs were prosecuted, and prior to World War I almost no one served time in prison for such crimes. Even to this day, virtually no whites have ever been punished for terrorizing blacks.

Lynch law was supposed to be, in the blunt words of one advocate of the practice, "the white woman's guarantee against rape by niggers." Ridding society of black brutes who violated Caucasian females was indeed the most frequently mentioned justification for lynching. But in fact, only about one third of all lynching victims were suspected of rape or attempted rape. Other possible transgressions ranged from something as serious as murder to something as foolish as "being uppity" or stealing chickens. Whatever the supposed crime, lynching was widely assumed to be a deterrent to black criminality. Lynching was a brutal business set out to protect the lives and rights of white Southerners, usually woman.

As I wrote the "White Folks'" stories, two questions continued to plague me. The first was, Who protected the black woman? Certainly not the black man, for as much as he wanted to protect his lady love, he was often powerless against the system. If he did make a stand, his own life would be in jeopardy, and his wife and children would be even more vulnerable. Nor could the black woman protect herself; she had neither the position nor the power. Instead she had to take whatever life dealt her and just learn to survive.

The second question that I grappled with was, Who protected the white woman from the white man? Her life was surely no picnic. I have heard many black women criticize the white woman of that time. She should have been stronger. She should have had sympathy for her black sisters. She should have done something, anything — anything at all. I thought much the same way until I began writing "Sara's Precious Babies." There is blame to be assigned, to be sure, but I've done some thinking and maybe grown up a little. Now I wonder if the white woman wasn't almost as much a victim of her environment as my women kin were of theirs, albeit her environment was filled with a little more finery and a few more trinkets. There are lots of pretty prisons, and I wouldn't want to live in any of them. Maybe these stories are just supposed to show that when it comes to brutality of any kind, there are often more victims than are apparent at first glance.

I know these stories aren't easy to read, but they are important because they provide a different perspective than is typically brought to the subject of lynching; they suggest that humanity can exist in the midst of brutality and that love can shine forth in the most difficult of circumstances. The husband and wife who comfort each other through the grief they share represent, for me, one of the finest examples of a loving relationship. The husband who holds his wife's hand, wipes away his own tears, and rocks a woman in his arms until she draws her last breath is the true strength of a black man. I would like to see more compassionate portrayals of black men as people tell their own stories — this aspect isn't explored nearly enough to suit me.

In these stories, folks suffer and move on. But like everything else in life, nothing that is deeply wounded — even after healing — remains as it was before.

Church Folks

Sister Mabel

Sister Mabel made her way slowly down the road to the church, trying ever so carefully not to mess up her new Sunday shoes. God, but it was hot today — over one hundred degrees. "It's just not supposed to get this hot in North Carolina, 'least not this early in the year, 'less the Devil gets to putting his hands in it. I just know this is some of his doing," she muttered resentfully. Lord, but this was an evil kind of heat, the kind that sneaks up on you and tries to kill you slowly. The kind that keeps you out of church when that's exactly where you need to be. The kind that's always looking to ruin a perfectly good Founder's Day.

But Satan was no match for Sister Mabel. She wasn't going to allow nothing or nobody to steal her joy. Even the church had been repainted, and it looked mighty fine, though it had been done piecemeal 'cause it was planting time. Bibleway Church certainly deserved no less, seeing how it was the oldest and most respected colored church in town.

Well, she had made it. She looked down quite proudly at her beautiful white shoes. Two miles, and not a single smudge. She still owed three dollars on these shoes, and she wanted them to last at least until they were paid for. Her mother always said that debt-ridden shoes would burn up your feet, and these almost had, she thought bitterly as she looked up at the blazing sun. She usually didn't get anything so frivolous on the book 'cause you never knew when you might need that credit for something that really mattered, like that fertilizer she'd ordered for her tomatoes last week. She was having it shipped all the way from up North, and if it came from up there then it had to be good.

She smiled an obligatory smile at two ladies standing by the great oak. She didn't recognize them right off, so she moved a bit closer to get a better look. Well, for goodness' sake — the hussies were both wearing work-stained day dresses, one of 'em was barefoot, and the other one had on turnover shoes. Both of them could have used a real good girdle, too, 'cause every time they moved, their hips shook up and down and then did a mean roll from side to side. It was simply shameful to see two grown women a-wiggling and a-jiggling all around the place like that. Didn't they know that there were some places that the Lord made fit to be tied or at the very least strapped down? Neither of 'em must've had a decent mama. Sister Mabel didn't know who was responsible for women like these being here, but she was certainly going to find out. How in the world were you supposed to trust a woman who didn't think enough to wear decent drawers or have sense enough to own respectable shoes?

Sister Mabel waved to Brother and Sister Holland. Sister Holland must have borrowed that money she was looking for to get her teeth fixed, because today she smiled a real big smile and Sister Mabel didn't see any snags. Even Sister Sophie looked like she was going to act like a decent human being today and listen to what somebody else had to say for a change. Let's just hope she keeps her mouth shut so we won't have to worry about the sunlight bouncing off those horrible gold teeth of hers, Sister Mabel silently prayed. It was so very distracting to those who were trying to enjoy the service. Oh, and there was Sister Williamson with her grandson. That hell-raising youngster needed everything the church could give him, and then some. Sister Mabel would be sure to have him seated on the mourning bench with all the other unsaved souls, and maybe, just maybe, if they all got together today, they might just be able to pray that boy's way to some better living.

She took a seat on her family's special pew. They were not just members of Bibleway but founding officers. The bench had been their very own since the church began. Her daddy had been the very first deacon and one of the few that could read every word in the Bible. It was a good thing, too, because it would be many a day that he would be called upon to point some heathen toward the path of righteousness.

The choir was looking good. They should do all right today. She'd spoken to the choir director and instructed him that there was to be none of that gut-bucket gospel today. She looked around and noticed that she didn't see Martha. That was good — maybe they would all be spared that shouting and moaning she insisted on. Why, she was so noisy last week that Sister Mabel had been tempted to stuff a handkerchief in her mouth, but how would it look if the head deaconess did something like that? Today maybe they would be able to worship in a dignified manner. You could never tell, the white folks might drop in for a spell. How would it look if they were all riled up like some backwoods fieldhands in a local praise-house? Sister Mabel just couldn't understand why Sister Martha didn't choose to conduct herself with the good graces the Savior gives a woman. All that bouncing and cutting up did nothing more than get you sweating like you was some kind of animal. Just last week, Martha got to running up and down the aisles till she almost flipped her two-dollar wig! Now, suppose the white folks had been there to see something like that? They never would get that donation for the building fund. Mister Jim promised he would stop by today, and if things went the way they were supposed to, there would be no telling what he would do for the church. If you just knew how to talk to the white folks, well, proper-like, then they could be all right. These colored folks round here wouldn't understand nothing like that, so best they didn't even know that he was coming. Best they just found out when he got here.

The Reverend looked quite nice. She nodded at him. He must've gone clear to Greenville to get that suit. She wondered if the church was supposed to pay for it. Oh well, it was Founder's Day, and if the sermon turned out to be as fine as the suit, then everybody would get their money's worth. He hadn't been her choice for a preacher, but she'd been outvoted. In retrospect, he could preach pretty fair, but Sister Mabel couldn't seem to forget that he'd showed up at their get-to-know-you luncheon in a light-blue jacket and brown shoes. What kind of preacher dressed like that? But today his shoes went with his suit, and it looked like everything was going to be quite fine indeed.

After the service today there would be iced tea and sandwiches in the basement, ideal refreshment for such a hot day, and a mite more civilized than the pig's-feet dinners she'd heard they'd served at Primitive Baptist last Sunday for their Founder's Day. She hadn't been there to see it for herself, but Sister Lou went and told her all about it — the slimy pig's feet and greasy tablecloths. Well, Sister Lou didn't actually say the tablecloths were greasy, but what else could they be with a menu like that? Some people just didn't understand the dignity required to truly serve the Father.

The preacher looked like he was ready to get started. Eleven o'clock, not a minute too soon or a minute too late. Perfect! He was standing nice and straight, too. That was good 'cause only a heathen slouched when they were trying to proclaim the Word, that's how you knew that they heathens! If you're proud to serve the Lord, well, then, you're supposed to look like it. Oh, a nice little prayer, too, a little long with a few too many hallelujahs thrown in, but all in all, quite appropriate. *I will lift up mine eyes unto the hills from whence cometh my help.* A good scripture to base a sermon on. A preacher could really go a long way with that one. The Reverend was really doing quite well for himself. A little joke thrown in for good measure — not that she liked to see a minister skinnin' and grinnin,' but a joke every once in a while wasn't too bad.

Go ahead and preach the word, Reverend, make us all proud. He was looking mighty good . . . oh no, wait a second, Sister Mabel thought nervously. He done detoured from the holy highway and was now heading down a dangerous road.

". . . and you busybody old women who think you know everything . . ."

I just knew it, Sister Mabel fumed. He done quit the preaching and took to meddling. That man just wouldn't stay put. Oh, well, at least he didn't usually preach too long, so he should be through directly, and not a moment too soon as far as Sister Mabel was concerned.

Brother Jake

Brother Jake looked up at the heavens and wondered if the Lord was looking down at him. He could be sure the Devil was looking up at him — that rascal seemed to be everywhere he was all of the time. No, it was the Lord that worried him. God just had to be looking, thought Brother Jake nervously, so that He could see that Jake was really here. Brother Jake needed all the points he could collect, and it wasn't too often that he came by for a visit, so if God wasn't looking today, there would be no telling when He would see Brother Jake this way again. Heavens, these seats were hard, this suit was too tight, and these shoes hurt like hell! Oops, was it a sin to be thinkin' hell, or was it all right as long as you didn't say it out loud? Brother Jake couldn't afford to be committing no wrongs, especially not in the church. He was here to be adding to the tally, not to be takin' nothin' away! Seemed like sittin' through this old lousy service ought to give a body a few bonus points. These folks singing didn't sound nothing like he'd remembered, and the preacher couldn't preach a lick! The Reverend wasn't hittin' on nothin', nothin' at all. A whole lot of big words and even more supposin'. Supposin' this and supposin' that. Suppose he just sat his black butt down? Now suppose that?

Why couldn't these fancy-dancy preachers just come on out and hit it straight, even if they got to use them a crooked stick? This man had to be new. He wasn't around the last time, Brother Jake was sure about that. 'Course that had been 'bout ten years ago, and a whole lot of folks done come and gone since then. Well, it didn't matter how bad it all was, this was where he needed to be. Time was passing on by, and he was getting old fast. It was more than a notion that it was time for him to be gettin' close to the Lord. He would need to be somewhere near Him if he was gonna get to Heaven — sure couldn't get there no other way, and that was exactly where he wanted to go. His mama was expectin' him to show up there sooner or later, and didn't no real man let down his mama. The Lord knew, too, that he'd already been to hell, and he sure wasn't lookin' to go there no more. Hell no! There was still a chance, though, that he'd be able to wrangle him a blessing here today, if only this preacher would say a little something he could grab on to. He wasn't going to worry yet, though, the service wasn't but half over!

Why couldn't that preacher up there preach him one of them sermons like Reverend Cole used to? Now that was a preaching man! If Brother Jake could just get something out of this here message, maybe then he'd have a prayer for getting into Heaven. This was one time somebody ought to shoot the messenger! Now if Reverend Cole had been up there, he would have made sure that Brother Jake got to where he needed to go. That man sure knew 'bout this Heaven and Hell thing, broke it down one time so everybody could see their way clear through. That sure was some sermon Reverend Cole preached that Sunday 'bout ten years ago. It was a lot better than this here. Yessirree, that was some sermon, some sermon indeed.

. . . Brothers, sisters, saints and sinners, you listening this morning to the words of the Lord as they pass through me, the Reverend James Cole, Sister Sue's baby boy. Today I'm gonna preach on the beautifulness of Heaven and the ugliness of Hell, and I suggest you listen up so you'll know what kind of a fix you might be in. Now I ain't figuring on being so late today that you rot where you sit, but I ain't fixing to shortchange the Lord, neither.

Now, 'bout this Heaven and Hell, there's a few things you needs to be understanding. Ya'll know if you look around you that all flesh ain't the same. You got the flesh of the whites and the flesh of the coloreds, and they different as different can be. Well, Heaven and Hell is set up the same way.

The Lord was pretty smart when it come to these things. That's why He ain't made the Heavens and the Hells exactly alike. He made a different Heaven and a different Hell for the different kinds of folks that live on this Earth. That way won't no one place get too crowded and there won't be no mixing of the races. So all of you coloreds who was figuring on breaking holy bread with the whites — there ain't gonna be none of that, so don't even be figuring on it. You ought to know that the white folks wouldn't be studying on nothing like that, and 'sides, the way they cook, you ain't gonna want none of their grub no way, and their music — Lord, have mercy, we ain't even gonna speak on that!

Now, our New Jerusalem ain't gonna be no coon town. No barbecues, fish frys, or Saturday-night frolics, but they'll be plenty of good food and time to take a rest. But some of ya'll ain't gonna get in 'less you stop your evil ways. When death comes knocking your gonna miss that train to glory. You can roll your eyes, stomp your feet, and poke out your lips all you want to, but it ain't gonna do you a bit of good. It won't get you nowhere except that place called "Hell" that stays about fifty below.

Yeah, that's the place you going if you don't do right — a place that freezes over all year long. A place where the Devil gonna say good morning by knocking you upside your head with snowballs. Now you think on that, you no-good, sin-filled benchwarmers. It's gonna be so cold that it's gonna freeze your lips shut! You ain't gonna be able to talk, not one word — that's torture for some of ya'all. You just remember this:

> *It rains and it hails.*
> *Snow coming down like the Devil poured it from a pail.*
> *But it's way too late to weep or cry 'cause*
> *the preacher told me this was where I'd be when I die. . . .*

Brother Jake remembered that sermon word for word. The best part came long after everybody was gone. He went up to Reverend Cole and asked him, "What kind of Heaven and Hell was you preaching 'bout, Reverend? I ain't never heard nothing like that before."

"Oh, Brother Jake, you know that I knows that the Bible says Hell is fire and brimstone, but then you know, too, that you can't be scaring no colored folks with hot weather. If you wants to get to 'em, then you got to be scaring them with freezing cold." And with that, Reverend Cole chuckled his way past Brother Jake and walked right out the door.

Brother Jake looked up at this here Reverend Jackson who was still struggling to make a point. It looked like there wasn't going to be a chance for him to earn his place in Heaven here today. He smiled as he thought about Reverend Cole again. No, they sure don't make 'em like that no more. No, they sure as hell don't!

Mister Jim

When Mister Jim walked in, he looked like a little piece of old cotton carelessly tossed onto a sea of darkened waters. He was late, too, real late, but better late than never. He walked right up to the front, though, right on through the middle of the service. Boy, there was something about white folks, you sure had to give 'em that. They may not have a single dime, or one ounce of usefulness, but you put 'em in a room full of Negroes, a room that rightfully belongs to the Negro, and that white man will march through like he's the first king. Well, Mister Jim must have attended that particular school of thought 'cause he guided hisself right on through the service and sat down front next to Miss Mabel on her special pew.

Normally Miss Mabel would act like a cat with her fur in a fix if anybody dared rest they britches on down next to hers, but this was Mister Jim, the white man come a-calling, so that meant it was OK. She smiled a real pretty smile, too. Folks made sure to study that smile real careful-like 'cause they couldn't be sure when they would see such a look 'cross Miss Mabel's face again.

Now, Mister Jim had planned it so he would be late. He figured he'd go ahead and miss the preachin' (what did a nigger know 'bout a Bible, anyway?), but he'd make sure he was in plenty of time for the singin'. Now, the niggers could sure enough sing, he would give them that. It was like the Lord had done something special to their voices, somethin' He ain't thought to do to the white folks'. It moved in places nobody could touch, and everybody else just paled in comparison. But the niggers, yessiree, now they could sing. And today being Founder's Day, they ought to sound real good. They sure had enough of 'em standing up there, too, enough of 'em to wake the dead and dying, too. He wondered if what he'd heard was true, that it was all the sorrow stored up in their souls that made a nigger sing like that. Well, if that was it, they ought to sing up a storm today. The way things were going for 'em in this here town ought to have 'em soundin' like they got them a jagged knife stuck in their guts. But wasn't none of that his problem. He couldn't be studying up on niggers' troubles; he had way too many of his own. All he had to be studyin' on was the singin' and givin' these folks a few dollars for their building fund. Hell, that was no problem; the singin' was worth that much! Man, could niggers sing!

Didn't nobody here know it, but this wasn't Mister Jim's first time in service with a colored church. Even Miss Mabel didn't know that. To be truthful, he'd never actually been inside one of their churches. He would never go that

225

far before. He'd simply stood underneath the window of this little colored church when he was a boy. With a daddy who was no-account and a mama who was a whore, his folks worshiped sin like some folks loved the Lord. Both of 'em got full into their cups every Saturday, stayed passed out clear through the night, and then pissed their way on through the Lord's day each and every week. Come Monday, he would never make it to school 'cause it would be up to him to clean up their mess. He hated it, but it was up to him to dust them off, feed 'em, and then help pick up their lives 'cause they sure as hell weren't able. He couldn't afford to let 'em kill themselves, least not till he was sure he didn't need 'em anymore.

'Course then all the other white folks would look at him like something the town dragged up from the ditch, and they sure weren't about to invite him into their proper little churches, and he wasn't about to beg nobody for his little piece of Jesus. So he snuck on over to the next town and made friends with all the little nigger children. Their mamas fed him and the boys understood him, 'cause some of them had daddies every bit as no-account as his. They finally made him see that only Jesus was supposed to bear another person's sins. So he let the little niggers give him a life, at least for a while, or at least until he could become a man.

And another church, one a lot like this one here, had been his salvation on some dark and lonely days. Sittin' here was almost like going home again, but that was a secret reserved only for Mister Jim and them that lived up in the heavenly skies. He was quality now and couldn't be bothering with no niggers. He had learned that they had

226

their place and he had his, and as long as folks stayed put, they could make it in this here town. It was when folks got turned around and tried to change the workings of the world that problems got started. 'Course Mister Jim didn't feel no shame about being among the niggers today. This was different; this was OK because afterward he would go back to where he belonged and they would stay here where *they* belonged. He would write them a small check, he was willing to help, but not too much. His folks would understand his charity — quality whites always gave the niggers a little something for their trouble from time to time. It was not only respected, but expected. If you got a hungry dog, you ain't got to feed him to hush him, just throw him a bone.

Mister Jim sat back in his seat and got himself ready to hear some good singin'. He listened for a moment, but then he started to frownin' like somebody was standin' right on his big toe. What in the world had happened to the niggers and the good singin'? These here sounded like some white folks howlin' at the moon. Well, it was time to go. If they were going to sing like this, then there simply wasn't no reason for him to stay. He smiled at Miss Mabel, pressed a check into her hands, and then once again walked straight on through the service, and on out the front door!

The Reverend

The reverend finished up his sermon with a resounding "Praise the Lord." As he seated himself, the choir director started playing "Going up Yonder." They was starting it off nice and kind of calm and slowly building up steam. In a few minutes, some sister would stand, clap her hands, and tap her feet. That feeling would soon start to spread, and then another soul would join in. Somebody else would shed a few tears, and one or two of them would moan softly in their seats. The spirit would go through that room, starting with just a spark here and there before engulfing them all in a full-blown fire.

The Reverend looked over at Miss Mabel and noticed that cold, hard look in her eyes. She was mad as the dickens, that was for sure. She obviously hadn't liked the sermon because she'd grimaced the whole way through. And she didn't like this singing, neither, because she was frowning like Satan himself had come to visit. No, Miss Mabel wasn't too happy, but the Reverend really didn't care. This was his church, and if he wanted to fuss out a few folks in his message, including her, well, that was between him and the Lord. There wasn't a thing she could do about it, neither. The Lord delivered the wisdom, not Miss Mabel, and thank God for that! And if he wanted to *hear* what she called "gut-bucket gospel," then he would. She would just have to deal with it. Mercy, she was really frowning now. Well, at least she'd seemed real pleased with his suit. Yeah, she did seem to like that.

The choir was singing like the Lord was working His way through them for sure. Some had their eyes closed and seemed to be in their own little world. He loved to watch the sisters especially. His wife didn't understand that one, but there was nothing sinful about his admiration. The sisters just had such deep feelings about things. They struggled so, too, but come Sunday morning they could let it all go, and they did, too, with power and grace.

He really needed them today. Needed their strength and their love, and he felt both as they sang and swayed. Yes, Lord, give me some of that power. Make this two-bit field-hand into one of your most blessed. He had fasted and he had prayed for a renewed spirit, and now the miracle had arrived. He bobbed his head to the beat. Lord, he was starting to feel good! He had walked in this morning feeling a little blue and very low down. But now he could feel the presence of greatness. The Lord had not forsaken them. He was here, right in the midst of the children who needed Him. Sister Martha was standing now — her shoes were already off, and her arms were making their way up high. She was getting ready, getting ready to fly. Go 'head, Sister Martha, he thought, you go ahead and just soar! He sat back now and got good and comfortable so he, too, could go along for the ride.

Hallelujah! Her heart was now healed,
and her worn soul had been made new.
Yet there was more to be said, even more for her to do.
The Lord had filled her with His great spirit
He had shown her His great love.
And like the never-ending waters springing forth like the
*   fountains,*
so the holy waters welled within her
ready to break through the now-weakened barriers.

She looked at the others, but they were bowed at the throne of
*   mercy,*
bound in their own thoughts, coping with their own pain.
The horn of Gabriel had summoned forth the fine saints
and Sister Martha answered His call.
She shouted!
Majestic and wondrous in her worship
She sang to Him exalting His fine praises.
How else could she thank Him for His goodness, His mercy
And this, another victory.
Her aged body became her temple
and the pews her points of penance.
The world stood silent before her
and her splendorous spiritual captivated them.
Her dignity, her power, her strength yet abound,
Sister Martha loved Him without a single solitary sound.
Her body, once crippled and ladened with pain
was now agile as a panther's and graceful as a gazelle's.

The Reverend

The sanctuary rolled out the red carpet,
for she was to fulfill a most blessed duty.
Her aisles became the tabernacle for the transition
and they all witnessed a most majestic worship.
Sister Martha's arms arched upward as she
reached for Him and twisted in His glory!
The tears had smoothed the wrinkles upon her cheeks
and she seemed ageless, the everlasting beauty.
She cared not for the invasion, because
they were not a part of this majesty.

This was a private performance for her Savior
her God and her blessed Lord.
She had asked Him for a blessing
and the Master had seen fit to grant her a reward.
How she must love Him,
and how He must love her.
And as Sister Martha danced
The Reverend couldn't help but thank Him.
Sister Martha danced not only for her redemption
and honor to His glory, but she danced ever so proudly
for His salvation and deliverance.
She was dancing for Him.

AFTERTHOUGHTS

The religious life and worship practices of many African Americans today are rooted in traditional African religions and white Protestant evangelism. Although a few slaves in Maryland and Louisiana were raised as Catholics, most

231

African Americans had virtually no contact with Catholicism and instead converted, in large numbers, to the Baptist and Methodist faiths in the late eighteenth century. The Baptists and the Methodists were attractive to enslaved Africans for three main reasons: 1) the emotional charge of the service reminded them of their African homes and their own native worship traditions; 2) many Baptists and Methodists claimed to be opposed to slavery and thus were associated with emancipation; and 3) the Baptist and Methodist churches licensed black men to preach.

By the 1780s, pioneer black ministers were already ministering to their own people in the South, and blacks were fairly well integrated into the Protestant religions. However, white men who preached love and brotherhood but practiced bigotry and hatred were still the norm. It was typical for the master to beat his slaves on Sunday before the service and then force them to attend church, where the message was that slavery was good and that to be dutiful to a white master was to be dutiful to God. Despite the obvious hypocrisies, which endured for generations, the enslaved Africans clung to their newfound Christianity and even held their own secret meetings and worship services within the slave community.

From the time of slavery to the present day, the church has continued to be the center of the African American community. It was the place that folks gathered to discuss important happenings and planned a course of action. It was the place you could come to share your burdens with your neighbor. It was the place where you left the injustices and injuries of the world in the hands of a higher power. It was the rock of Gibraltar, a place to hold on to and a place to let go. In over three hundred years, the African American hasn't found a better place for maintenance of the soul.

They come for different reasons. They are looking to receive all kinds of blessings, bringing with them a range of life experiences. The characters in "Church Folks" symbolically represent this very scenario — different hopes for different folks coming together on a common ground. The poetic tribute at the end of the service is a testament to the intensity of the experience. It is joyous, it is sorrowful. It is soothing, it is powerful. It whispers, and then again it shouts. It makes you laugh and it moves you to tears. It's elevating and it's humbling. You never know what to expect from the black church, but there's a comfort in knowing that it's always there.

A Final Say

So, what is this book about? It's about the extraordinary lives of some pretty ordinary folks. It's about an appreciation for the words, wit, and wisdom from yesterday that help make sense of a chaotic today. It's a thank-you from an African American woman to some pretty awe-inspiring colored women. And it's about folk culture as a continuum, a link back to the essence of who we are and how we came to be.

This is also a wake-up call to some people I know, who in their desire to escape those difficult days and hard-to-survive places have foolishly thought they could leave their souls behind along with some of that pain, and then re-create themselves as they see fit. Well, we may run, but we can't hide, not from ourselves, not ever. And what's more, we shouldn't want to. Our heritage is a badge of honor that represents strength and survival. It should be given the respect it deserves.

Finally, this book is about multicultural education. It's

about letting some good people into a place they've never before been invited to enter. This book is a good look at everyday living, and to really understand folks, that's the kind of view you have to have.

My quest to become the kind of woman my grandma-mas would be proud of has been a long and difficult journey. It has meant taking off that mask of middle-class pretentiousness and dropping that "me generation" crap from my realm of consciousness. It has meant going back to some basic wisdom that is getting increasingly difficult to find but that, once recovered, is certainly worthy of praise. For me, the significance of my work is the ability to give voice to those very truths, and I have tried to do just that.

I have one final truth to leave with you. Every year we go back to the homeplace in Farmville, North Carolina. Driving by the old shacks, tobacco barns, and chicken coops always triggered an emotional response in me, but those were feelings that I couldn't quite articulate or explain. Now I live just a few miles from that place, and it's finally beginning to make sense. Maybe that's why I had to come back.

From the porch steps of a dilapidated old house, all the eye can see is the leftovers and leavings of some pretty hard living. To the casual observer, there isn't much around to smile about, but for the understanding soul, there're more wonders than the eye will ever see, and there's joy here, too — absolute and awe-inspiring joy. It took me years to figure out where that joy came from when, like so many ignorant others, all I could see was pain. I wondered, how did these folks manage to feel so happy in the midst of such difficult living? What did they know that we spoiled folks today can't seem to understand? And then it came to me. Came to me loud and clear, and I thanked God for the blessing. Granddaddy stepped into my consciousness one day and gave it to me straight up, and it made all the sense in the world. Yessirree, all the sense in the world.

I reckon that it's good, so good to be faithful.
It's plain comfortin' to know that you got you this one
who doesn't mind at all, not the least little bit,
of catching you when you fall, or steadyin' you when you stumble
or remindin' us always that we ain't nothin' but human
so we'd best to be humble.
And then, then when them times come down oh so hard
And them days come to call that sho' 'nough get too tough
I still got me somebody
who loves me — yes, loves me
No matter what!

I reckon it's sweet, so sweet to just know
that all I can see ain't all that there be.
And these lousy old folks round here that I see,
sure gonna get 'em, all they got due 'em,
and thankfully, it ain't up to me to study up how,
how to give it straight to 'em.

Oh, ain't it good, so good to be faithful
'cause it a wonder, yessirree,
that someone done thought of someone like me
to give me all this here,
this here that I got.

And then went to figurin' a tree in that spot.
And look at that flower, that beautiful flower
right in a spot that needed a flower,
and that same one will love it, well enough don't you see?
To send down the rains in a joyous spring shower.

Mercy, ain't it good, so good to be faithful
'cause I know it won't be long
till I'll hoe my last field beneath the hot blazin' sun
and still it won't be over.
It will be WELL DONE! WELL DONE! WELL DONE!

Oh, ain't it good to be faithful
'cause there sho' been some times,
some of 'em pretty darn bad
when a little bit of faith was all we colored folks had.
But baby, I can tell you, tell you how it's been true,
that it's good to be faithful. I know it, I do.
It's just good to be faithful, so good,
Lord, let me tell you!

Acknowledgments

I would like to acknowledge several people who contributed to this project. First, I would like to recognize my original publisher, Summerhouse Press, which first appreciated the merit of my message. Second, I would like to thank the wonderful team at Little, Brown and Company who appreciated the possibilities, shared the vision, and then worked so hard to make an author's greatest dreams come true. A special thanks goes to Jonathan Greene for the artwork that adorns the cover. He is a generous soul, and his creative genius has been a blessing to this book. Finally, I would like to thank Carroll Greene, Dr. Patricia Stewart, and Dr. Barbara Fertig of Savannah, Georgia, for their love and support. Also hats off to my agent, Carol Mann of New York, New York, who held my hand and assured me again and again that things always work out just the way they are supposed to. Thank you, one and all.